ONE DAMN MISTAKE

Fargo unfurled and stood with his elbow and brushing his holster. "I'm saying you're the curs. And you're welcome to stand up and prove me wrong."

"You're proddin' us—is that it?" Alonzo said.

"He *is* an Injun lover," Milton said as if it astonished him.

Alonzo nodded. "Mister, we thank you for showin' your hand. You could have just gunned down the five of us in the middle of the night."

"Five?" Fargo said, and spiked with alarm.

"That's the other reason we shot those heathens," Alonzo said. "One of us had his horse crippled by a fall and we needed an animal for him to ride." He smiled and looked past Fargo. "Ain't that right, Willard?"

"It sure as hell is," said a gruff voice behind Fargo even as a gun muzzle was jammed against the back of his head . . .

HIGH COUNTRY GREED

by

Jon Sharpe

A SIGNET BOOK

SIGNET
Published by New American Library, a division of
Penguin Group (USA) Inc., 375 Hudson Street,
New York, New York 10014, USA
Penguin Group (Canada), 90 Eglinton Avenue East, Suite 700, Toronto,
Ontario M4P 2Y3, Canada (a division of Pearson Penguin Canada Inc.)
Penguin Books Ltd., 80 Strand, London WC2R 0RL, England
Penguin Ireland, 25 St. Stephen's Green, Dublin 2,
Ireland (a division of Penguin Books Ltd.)
Penguin Group (Australia), 250 Camberwell Road, Camberwell, Victoria 3124,
Australia (a division of Pearson Australia Group Pty. Ltd.)
Penguin Books India Pvt. Ltd., 11 Community Centre, Panchsheel Park,
New Delhi - 110 017, India
Penguin Group (NZ), 67 Apollo Drive, Rosedale, Auckland 0632,
New Zealand (a division of Pearson New Zealand Ltd.)
Penguin Books (South Africa) (Pty.) Ltd., 24 Sturdee Avenue,
Rosebank, Johannesburg 2196, South Africa

Penguin Books Ltd., Registered Offices:
80 Strand, London WC2R 0RL, England

First published by Signet, an imprint of New American Library,
a division of Penguin Group (USA) Inc.

First Printing, March 2012
10 9 8 7 6 5 4 3 2 1

The first chapter of this book previously appeared in *Rocky Mountain Ruckus*, the
three hundred sixty-fourth volume in this series.

Copyright © Penguin Group (USA) Inc., 2012
All rights reserved

 REGISTERED TRADEMARK—MARCA REGISTRADA

Printed in the United States of America

The Trailsman

Beginnings ... they bend the tree and they mark the man. Skye Fargo was born when he was eighteen. Terror was his midwife, vengeance his first cry. Killing spawned Skye Fargo, ruthless, cold-blooded murder. Out of the acrid smoke of gunpowder still hanging in the air, he rose, cried out a promise never forgotten.

The Trailsman they began to call him all across the West: searcher, scout, hunter, the man who could see where others only looked, his skills for hire but not his soul, the man who lived each day to the fullest, yet trailed each tomorrow. Skye Fargo, the Trailsman, the seeker who could take the wildness of a land and the wanting of a woman and make them his own.

High in the Rockies, 1861—a wild town where greed is the way of life and a pack of killers runs roughshod.

1

Buzzards led Fargo to the bodies. He was bound for the Rockies and happened to gaze into the sky to the south and there they were, half a dozen large black V's winging in close circles. It could have been anything that brought them. A dead animal was most likely.

Fargo was far from any settlements and there wasn't a farm or a ranch within hundreds of miles. But he had a hunch and he had learned long ago not to ignore his gut instincts.

Reining the Ovaro toward the carrion eaters, he loosened the Colt in its holster.

Fargo was a big man. He nearly always wore buckskins and always had a red bandanna around his throat. His boots were scuffed, his spurs well worn. Jutting from his saddle scabbard was the stock of a Henry rifle. In his boot he had an Arkansas toothpick.

His piercing lake-blue eyes took in everything. Only a fool let down his guard in the wild and Fargo was no fool.

This was Indian country, mainly Cheyenne and Arapaho. A few months ago a treaty had been signed that would put them on reservations and open the land to whites. Neither tribe was happy about it. They argued that the government had tricked a handful of leaders into signing the treaty without the consent of the rest.

Fargo came to a low rise and saw the bodies. There were two, sprawled belly down in the grotesque postures of death. Both wore buckskins. As he approached he saw that both had black hair past their shoulders and wore moccasins.

"Hell," Fargo said.

Rising in the stirrups he scanned the prairie in all directions.

Other than a few antelope to the northwest—and the vultures—he was the only living creature.

He rode in a circle around the dead warriors. Tracks showed where five riders on shod mounts had come out of the south. More tracks showed where the five shod mounts went off to the west, leading two unshod horses.

The killers had made no attempt to hide their sign.

His saddle creaking under him, Fargo dismounted. Few flies had gathered, which told him the bodies hadn't been there long. Using the tip of his right boot, he rolled one over.

It was a young Arapaho who had barely seen twenty winters. A slug had taken him in the left eye and exited out his right temple. The other one had been shot in the forehead. Neither had been mutilated.

Fargo gazed to the west. The five whites who killed the warriors were heading toward the far-distant Rockies. He took up their trail.

Fargo wasn't the law. He had no legal right to go after them. But he'd like to know why they did it.

Had the warriors attacked them? Or was it something else?

It was common for a lot of whites to hate the red man simply because Indians were red and for a lot of Indians to hate the white man because the white man wasn't red.

Fargo couldn't abide the haters on either side.

Before him stretched the vast prairie. So much space, you'd think the white man and the red man could live on it in peace, but that would never be.

A sentinel prairie dog atop its burrow whistled shrilly and the whole town scurried for cover.

Fargo reined wide of the mounds and the holes. He was too fond of the Ovaro to risk a busted leg.

The sun was hot, the smell of the grass and the earth always in his nose. He came on a trickle of a creek with banks three feet high. The bottom was choked with brambles and brush. He started down and spooked a small black bear that bolted up the other side and stopped to stare in bewilderment, and snort. He laughed, and the bear loped along the bank and disappeared into more growth.

A half mile on and he spooked a rabbit. It bounded twenty

yards or so and stopped to glance back and see if he was after it. He almost shucked the Henry to have rabbit stew for supper. But hardly did the notion cross his mind than the air whistled to the streak of a feathered predator and a hawk dived out of the clear blue. There was a frightened squeal and a brief flutter of wings and a thrashing of legs, and the rabbit lay limp. The hawk looked at him, tilting its head from side to side, as if daring him to try to steal its meal.

"It's all yours," Fargo said.

A thin bowl of sun was all that was left when Fargo spied gray snakes coiling into the sky. He put his hand on his Colt and went on at a walk.

Their fire was too big, a common mistake of those green behind the ears. They were seated around it jawing and drinking coffee and must have had their ears stopped with wax because they didn't hear him until he was almost on top of them.

There were four, not five. Fargo figured the tracks of the fifth shod horse belonged to a pack animal.

Suddenly one of them bleated a warning and all four grabbed rifles and sprang to their feet with the alacrity of men who feared they might take arrows.

"Howdy, gents," Fargo said amiably as he drew rein. He leaned on his saddle horn. "Saw your fire and reckoned you might share a cup."

All four were middling in age, which surprised Fargo; he'd thought they would be younger. Two had bristly beards and two didn't. Their clothes were a mix of homespun and store-bought that had seen better days. Only two wore revolvers but all of them had rifles and knives.

"Damn it to hell, mister," the bulkier of the bearded pair exclaimed. "You shouldn't ought to sneak up on folks like that."

Fargo gestured at the open prairie. "You call this sneaking?"

A smooth-chinned rake handle with tufts of hair poking out of his ears chortled. "He's got you there, Rafer. That we didn't see him is our own damn fault."

"We were damn careless," said the other bearded specimen.

"I reckon so, Milton," hairy-ears said.

3

"Can I light or not?" Fargo asked, and when the man called Milton nodded, he slid off and stretched.

"Been ridin' a far piece, have you?" asked hairy-ears.

"Clear from Saint Louis," Fargo said. He let the reins dangle and rummaged in a saddlebag for his tin cup. "How about you gents?"

"We're from down Kansas way," said hairy-ears. "My name is Alonzo, by the way." He pointed at the last of them, whose chin was cleft so deeply he appeared to have two. "And that there is Elias."

Fargo stepped to their fire. The coffeepot was half full. He filled his cup, took a step back, and squatted. "I take it by your clothes you must be farmers."

Alonzo bobbed his head. "That we are. Although maybe it should rightly be that we *were*. We've given up the plow to get rich."

"Are you fixing to rob banks?"

Alonzo laughed. Hunkering, he rested his rifle across his thighs. "I would if I thought we could get away with it. But I ain't hankerin' to be guest of honor at a strangulation jig."

"I bet we could do it," Rafer said. "We're smarter than most who pin on badges."

"We'd strike fast, then hide way off where no one is liable to find us." Milton added his two bits. "We're real good at livin' off the land."

"How are you at killing Indians?" Fargo casually threw in. He sipped and stared into his cup and when he looked up, all four were staring at him as if he were a rattler about to bite.

"Why'd you want to bring up a thing like that?" Alonzo asked.

"I came across a couple of Arapaho warriors a ways back," Fargo said. "Someone did them in."

"You're not an Injun lover, are you?" Milton asked suspiciously.

"Because if you are, we'll have no truck with you," Rafer declared.

Fargo nodded at their horse string. "Did you kill them for their animals?"

"Not just for that, no," Alonzo said, and scratched a hairy

4

ear. "We killed 'em mainly because they were redskins. Now we're bound for Denver."

"Then it's on to the mountains where we aim to strike it rich," Elias said.

Milton nodded. "Why, they say folks are pickin' the stuff right off the ground. Gold nuggets as big as your fist."

"Or maybe we'll find silver," Elias said excitedly.

"We hear tell they've found veins of it as wide as a Conestoga."

"Can you imagine?" Milton said.

Fargo sipped and smiled and said, "Idiots could."

Their friendly smiles faded and Rafer growled, "What was that about idiots?"

"I've been to the Rockies more times than you have fingers and toes," Fargo said. "There's gold, and there's silver, but it's not lying on the ground and the veins are hard to find. If it was easy, every mother's son as stupid as you four would be rolling in money, but most end up broke or dead or both."

"You just called us stupid," Milton said.

"What else would you call someone who shot two Indians for no reason?"

"Hold on now," Alonzo bristled. "They were red. What more reason does anyone need?"

"Were they out to lift your hair?"

"No, they was just ridin' along," Alonzo said. "They even acted friendly when we rode up but we didn't pay them no never mind and shot them down."

"Red curs," Rafer growled.

Alonzo nodded.

Milton showed most of his teeth in a happy grin and exclaimed, "They never knew what hit 'em."

"What about their women?" Fargo brought up. "What about their kids?"

Alonzo's dark eyes narrowed. "What the hell is wrong with you, mister? Are you white or what? Who cares if they had women or sprouts? They were *Injuns*. Dirty, filthy, stinkin' redskin Injuns."

"I was afraid that's how it was," Fargo said wearily. He sighed and set his cup on the ground so his hands were free for what came next.

"Why afraid?" Alonzo asked.

"Because I am sick to death of peckerwoods like you," Fargo told him. "Because now you have stepped in it and there's no way out."

"What the hell are you talkin' about?" Rafer demanded.

Fargo unfurled and stood with his right hand brushing his holster. "I'm saying you're the curs. And you're welcome to stand up and prove me wrong."

"You're proddin' us—is that it?" Alonzo said.

"He *is* an Injun lover," Milton said as if it astonished him.

"Well, I reckon we know what we have to do," Rafer remarked.

Alonzo nodded. "Mister, we thank you for showin' your hand. You could have just gunned down the five of us in the middle of the night."

"Five?" Fargo said, and spiked with alarm.

"That's the other reason we shot those heathens," Alonzo said. "One of us had his horse crippled by a fall and we needed an animal for him to ride." He smiled and looked past Fargo. "Ain't that right, Willard?"

"It sure as hell is," said a gruff voice behind Fargo even as a gun muzzle was jammed against the back of his head.

2

Willard was a big 'un, as they'd say. He reached around Fargo with an arm twice as wide as Fargo's and snatched the Colt from its holster, saying, "You won't be needin' this, mister."

Fargo grabbed the man's wrist and whirled, or tried to. A blow to the back of his head caused the world to explode in pinwheels of bright light and he pitched to his hands and knees and almost blacked out.

"Behave now, you hear, Injun lover?" Willard warned. "Next time I'll cave in your damn skull."

Fighting dizziness and nausea, Fargo looked up.

Willard was a walking slab of muscles in a rumpled shirt and baggy pants with red suspenders. On his big head was a small straw hat with a frayed brim. He grinned and said, "I didn't like you tryin' to rile my friends like that to give you an excuse to shoot them."

"It was damned impolite," Alonzo said.

"The question is," Elias broke in, "what do we do with him?"

Rafer patted his rifle. "You know what my vote will be. The only thing I hate worse than Injuns are whites who don't know the color of their own skin."

"I hear that," Milton said. "Maybe we should do to him as we done to those redskins."

Elias regarded Fargo gravely. "I don't know as I cotton to killin' a white man. It ain't the same as snuffin' red vermin."

"Injun lovers and Injuns are the same, I tell you," Rafer said belligerently.

"I'm with Elias on this," Alonzo said. "I don't like what this feller did but he *is* white and that has to count for somethin'."

"Hell," Rafer grumbled. "What do you say, Willard?"

Willard was holding a revolver in each hand. He hefted

Fargo's Colt and said, "He didn't hurt any of us although I suspect that was his intention. I say we let him off easy this time, but this time only. If'n he gives us trouble later, we buck the son of a bitch out in lead."

By then Fargo's head had cleared enough that he could say, "All of you can go to hell."

"Will you listen to him?" Alonzo marveled. "We have him over a barrel and he thinks he's a snappin' turtle."

"Kill him," Rafer urged.

"No," Willard said. "But we won't let him come after us, neither. We'll tie him good and tight and leave him. If'n he gets loose, fine. If'n he don't, why, that's fine, too."

Alonzo and Elias liked that idea, and since Rafer and Milton were outvoted, Fargo got to live. But under cover of Willard's revolver, they cut short pieces from his own rope and bound his hands behind his back and tied his ankles, as well. Rafer did the wrists and he wound the rope so tight, Fargo's circulation was cut off. In no time his hands were near numb.

"We'll just leave you like this until mornin'," Willard said, "and then we'll be on our way."

"Let's help ourselves to his poke if he has one," Rafer suggested.

"No," Alonzo said. "What's the matter with you? Next thing we know, you two will be turnin' us into outlaws."

Elias said, "We're normal folks and I aim to stay normal."

Fargo was mad as hell. He tried to move his arms to get the blood flowing, and couldn't. "You tied me too damn tight."

"Aw, poor infant," Rafer said.

"That's just too bad, mister," Willard said. "But you ain't gettin' untied so you might as well just lie there and keep quiet or we'll gag you."

"Let's gag him anyhow," Milton said.

Rafer chortled and opened a saddlebag and brought out a wadded filthy sock. "This will do right fine."

"Try it and I'll bite your goddamn fingers off," Fargo said.

Without warning Willard stepped over and kicked Fargo in the side. A keg of black powder went off in his ribs. Doubling over, he nearly succumbed to agonizing waves of pain.

"That'll be enough out of you," Willard warned. "One more peep and Rafer gets to stick that dirty old sock of his clear down in your throat."

"You mean I can't?" Rafer said.

"If'n I was trussed up, I'd be angry too," Willard said. "So we'll overlook this once."

"You're too damn nice," Rafer complained. "This bastard lives, he'll come after us and you'll be sorry you didn't listen to me and kill him when we could." Reluctantly, he placed the sock back in his saddlebag.

Fargo grit his teeth against the pain, and fumed. For once he agreed with Rafer. He *would* go after them and he *would* hold them to account for what they had done.

"How about we commence cookin' our supper?" Elias said. "I'm hungry enough to eat a bear."

"All we got is rabbit," Alonzo said, and held up one they must have shot earlier. Drawing his hip knife, he speared the tip into its belly. "I'll do the honors but tomorrow night someone else takes a turn."

"I expect Willard will want to feed this bastard, too," Rafer said.

"I was you," Willard said, "I wouldn't poke at me so much. I don't like it, not even a little bit."

"You better listen, Rafer," Elias said. "Willard stomped you once. He can do it again."

Rafer's face was ugly with resentment. "I was only sayin'."

Fargo had to lie there and listen to them bicker. If there was any feeling worse than being helpless, he had yet to experience it.

When the rabbit was cooked they passed out pieces but gave none to him. He was so hungry his stomach rumbled.

Rafer heard and grinned. "You hear that, boys? Our Injun lover has an empty belly."

"Too bad for him," Milton said. Biting lustily into his piece, he chewed and grinned at Fargo.

"We should feed him," Elias said.

"Like hell," Rafer returned.

"It's the Christian thing to do."

"I ain't as Christian as you and I say he doesn't get a nibble."

"You don't need to be so hard all the time," Elias said.

"It's a hard world. Those that are soft get ate like this rabbit."

"I'm giving him a piece," Elias said.

"Like hell you are."

"There's barely enough for the five of us." Willard put an end to their argument. "He goes hungry."

"I wish there was a better way," Elias said. "But I'll back whatever you want to do."

They took turns keeping watch. Milton was first. He kept rubbing his bulbous nose as if it itched and paid no attention to Fargo whatsoever.

Alonzo was next. He sat sipping coffee and admiring the sparkling plentitude of stars. At one point he looked at Fargo and said, "I bet you're sorry you made a fuss over them redskins, huh?"

"Go to hell."

"Now see. I'm tryin' to be civil and you throw it in my face."

Alonzo said no more and when his two hours were up he woke Rafer.

By then fatigue was gnawing at Fargo and he drifted off. It couldn't have been but a couple of minutes later that a sharp pain in his neck woke him and he jerked his head up with a start.

Rafer laughed. He was holding one of the sticks they'd used to skewer the rabbit meat. "Can't you sleep?" he said, and laughed.

Fargo realized the bastard had poked him with the stick. "You're real brave when a man's hands are tied."

"I'd do the same if they weren't," Rafer declared. "Don't you think I wouldn't." He waggled the stick. "I ain't lettin' you sleep a lick. You do, I'll jab you. Maybe next time it'll be in the eye."

Fargo's fury got the better of him. "You're one miserable son of a bitch." He braced for another poke or a kick but Rafer surprised him by chuckling.

"I suppose you would think that. But if you were like us and not a stinkin' Injun lover you'd find me right pleasant."

Fargo struggled to stay awake. Each time sleep threatened to overcome him, he imagined that stick piercing an eye. It helped to ward it off.

At last Rafer's turn was over. He woke Elias and crawled under his blankets.

Elias tended the fire and got up and checked on the horses and came back and squatted with his cup in his hands. He blew on the hot coffee and looked at Fargo and said, "I'm sorry about all this, mister."

"Cut me loose."

"I can't. I'd like to but they're my pards and I can't go against them."

"You could if you wanted," Fargo said.

"We have a policy, you might call it," Elias said. "We put everythin' to a vote and the majority always rules. Most of them want you trussed so that's how you'll stay."

"You're as worthless as they are."

"Here now," Elias said. "I stuck up for you, didn't I?" He glanced at the others and lowered his voice. "Tell you what I'll do." He set down his cup and drew his knife and cut a slice of rabbit meat from a stick lying half in the flames. "Here. Someone didn't finish this. You might as well have it."

The meat was near black but it was a good half inch thick. Fargo was so starved he wolfed it down and regretted his haste. He should have chewed a while and savored the taste.

Elias also gave him water. "That's the best I can do. I'm sorry. You'll have to bear it until you can free yourself."

Fargo had an ace up his sleeve, or rather, up his pant leg: the Arkansas toothpick. But he couldn't get at it with them watching. And besides he couldn't move his fingers.

Willard had the last watch. He hunkered, an immovable mountain, and ignored Fargo until shortly before dawn when he cleared his throat. "We'll be headin' out soon. We'll leave you your horse and put your smoke wagon in your saddlebags."

"If you expect me to thank you, you can wait until hell freezes over."

"Your skin saved you this once but it won't twice. If you're smart, this ends here. Come after us and you'll be sorry."

Fargo vowed then and there that as soon as he was free, that was exactly what he was going to do.

3

The five farmers who would be rich left at first light. Little was said. They gathered their effects and saddled their animals and climbed on.

Rafer was last. He came over to Fargo, smirked, and kicked him in the side.

Fargo sensed what he was about to do and doubled up to protect himself but it still hurt like hell and he let out a grunt.

Rafer drew back his leg to kick him again.

"No more of that," Willard said. "Only a spineless dog stomps a man when he's helpless."

"You callin' me yellow?" Rafer said.

"Get on your damn horse." Willard brought his own over and stared down at Fargo. "Remember what I told you. Don't be stupid."

To Fargo nothing was stupider than beating and binding a man—and leaving him alive. But he didn't tell the hulking farmer that. All he said was, "I've learned a lesson, that's for sure."

"Good." Willard misconstrued. "You can set to work on those ropes as soon as we're out of sight. It shouldn't take you more than five or six hours."

"What if he can't free himself?" Elias said. "He'll lie there until he starves or dies of thirst."

"Or a bear eats him," Milton said, sounding happy at the prospect.

Rafer had climbed on his mount. "Me, I hope redskins find him and stake him out and peel his hide. It would serve him right for bein' an Injun lover."

"Enough jabber," Willard said. Wheeling his sorrel, he rode off to the west.

The rest were quick to catch up. Raising puffs of dust, they dwindled into the distance and were swallowed by the morning haze.

Fargo didn't wait until they were out of sight. The moment they gigged their mounts, he tried to pry at the rope around his ankles. He was seeking to loosen the rope enough that he could slip his hand into his boot. His fingers, though, wouldn't cooperate. Frustrated, he tried to wriggle them. It hurt abominably but he refused to give up. He kept at it and kept at it and after a considerable while he was rewarded by being able to bend them a little.

Fargo was so intent on his hands that when the Ovaro nickered he didn't look up.

Then the stallion stomped a hoof and whinnied louder. It was tied to a picket pin, courtesy of Elias. Rafer had demanded to know why Elias bothered and mentioned that maybe it would drift off and leave Fargo afoot. Elias had replied that if it did stray off, Indians might find it, and he didn't want so fine an animal falling into red hands.

Fargo gazed in the direction the Ovaro was staring. All he saw were a few patches of heavy brush. He resumed his prying at the rope and had loosened it to where he almost had the coils above his boot when the Ovaro stamped and whinnied yet again.

Fargo looked and still didn't see why the stallion was agitated. He was about to bend to the rope when a hint of tawny movement sent a tingle down his spine. Something was slinking toward them, about fifty yards away. At first he thought it was a coyote, which didn't worry him too much. Loud shouts and a few kicks if it came close should drive it off. Then it raised its head and he saw the twin triangles of its ears and its round face and he knew what it really was—a cougar—and suddenly he was very worried.

Fargo swore and attacked the rope anew. It was rare to encounter one of the big cats, rarer still that a cougar would stalk a man in broad daylight. Then again, maybe it was the Ovaro the cougar was after. Normally the stallion was a match for any meat-eater this side of a grizzly, but picketed as it was, the cat had an edge.

Gritting his teeth, Fargo tugged and pulled. Another wrench

and his pant leg was above his boot. Quickly, he plunged his fingers in. The toothpick's hilt molded to his palm. He slid it out, reversed his grip, and sliced at the rope around his wrists. It was awkward and painful holding the knife that way but the discomfort was minor compared to what the cougar would do. He sliced and sliced. Beads of sweat broke out on his brow. His arms and shoulders throbbed.

The stallion stamped again.

The cat wasn't a dozen feet away. Its long tail twitching, it laid back its ears and snarled.

Fargo pressed the blade harder, his eyes on the cougar. It advanced slowly, moving one forepaw and then the other. Its slanted eyes were fixed on the Ovaro.

The stallion whinnied and bobbed its head and stomped, raising puffs of dust.

Try as Fargo could, the rope wouldn't part.

Suddenly the cat screeched and flew at the Ovaro. The stallion reared as high as it could and struck out with both front hooves. Instantly, the cougar sprang aside and came at the Ovaro again. A flashing paw narrowly missed the stallion's leg.

Fargo was beside himself. He strained, his wrists welters of agony. The rope parted. His hands were free. Quickly, he bent to the rope around his legs.

The cougar was trying to dart in and close with the Ovaro but so far the stallion's flashing hooves had held it at bay. Taking a long bound to one side, it tried to come at the Ovaro broadside but the Ovaro turned just enough to drive it back.

The picket pin was jerking and moving but was still limiting the stallion's movements.

The second rope fell away. Fargo heaved to his feet and took a step to go to the Ovaro's aid. His legs were so stiff from being tied so long that he stumbled and almost pitched onto his face. Recovering, he hopped and scrambled to the picket pin and slashed.

The Ovaro wheeled to confront the cat just as the cougar sprang at its flank. A hoof caught the meat-eater across the shoulder, sending it tumbling.

Fargo leaped for his saddlebags but the Ovaro was kicking and prancing. He tried for the scabbard, instead, and succeeded in grabbing the Henry's stock. But before he could pull it out, the stallion moved and he lost his hold.

The cougar crouched and hissed. Enraged by its failure to bring the Ovaro down, it let out an unearthly shriek.

A flailing hoof missed its head by inches.

Cougars were deadly killers but they weren't always tenacious. If prey fought back, if there was a chance of their being hurt, they would break off the fight and flee.

And that's exactly what this one did. Turning, it sped for the thick brush in long leaps that no other animal could match.

Fargo yanked the Henry from the saddle scabbard. He jammed it to his shoulder and fixed a quick bead but before he could fire the cougar made it to cover.

"Damn."

Fargo stood there, hoping the cat showed itself. Only after a couple of minutes went by and he was sure it was gone did he relax.

Fargo opened his saddlebag and took out his Colt. At least the bastards hadn't taken his guns. If they thought that would lessen the sting of what they had done, they were wrong.

In fifteen minutes Fargo was on their trail. They had too big a lead for him to overtake them quickly, but overtake them he would, if it took a month of Sundays.

Some might say he should let it go, that he'd brought it on himself by tracking them down, that the dead Arapahos meant nothing to him, and he was sticking his nose where it didn't belong. Maybe all that was true. But for what the farmers had done to him, there would be a reckoning.

They were pushing at a good clip. At times they galloped. At other times they slowed to a walk to let their horses catch their wind.

They were eager to strike it rich, these five. Fargo had run across more fools like them than he cared to count. Gold and silver strikes always brought them in droves, flushed with money fever, not caring a whit that the odds of becoming rich were slim to none. Only a few ever succeeded. Most worked their fingers to the bone for little more than enough to keep food in their bellies so they could go on scraping by.

To Fargo's way of thinking, chasing golden rainbows was

plumb stupid. You wouldn't catch him grabbing a pan and a pick and running off to the next big strike.

Night came, and he hadn't gained.

Fargo made camp in an old buffalo wallow, the stink long since gone. It hid his small fire. He drank piping hot coffee and chewed pemmican from a bundle he had in his saddlebags and listened to the lonesome laments of coyotes and wolves. Once he heard the roar of a bear. A griz, unless he was mistaken, as fearsome a brute as any creature on earth.

Daybreak found him on the Ovaro's hurricane deck, pushing westward. By early afternoon dark clouds were scuttling in, at first singly but soon in clusters and banks until the sky was overcast from end to end.

Fargo knew what was coming and sought shelter in a stand of cottonwoods.

Nature's tantrum lasted hours. It was a real gulley whomper, the wind howling, the rain so heavy it fell in sheets. Lightning seared the darkness and thunder cannonaded and the ground seemed to shake.

Fargo was spared the worst of it but he was still drenched by the time the storm ended. He climbed on the Ovaro and touched his spurs but now there were no tracks to follow; the storm had obliterated them.

That was all right, Fargo reflected. The five would keep on to the west, and the Rockies. Sooner or later he'd come across them again.

It was the next morning, when he had been in the saddle about an hour, that he happened to glance back and thought he saw riders far back. He blinked and they were gone. Although he looked for them throughout the day he didn't see them again.

That night he slept in peace.

Up at the crack of dawn, he pushed until noon, rested for half an hour, and was in the saddle again. Toward twilight he spotted several buffalo. Ordinarily he might drop one and dry the meat but he didn't have the time to spare.

About the middle of the next morning he drew rein at a log trading post.

An old coon by the name of Sublette owned it. The post

had been there since the beaver days, and did good business with the Indians.

Sublette, who sported a white beard down to his waist, nodded when Fargo asked about the five farmers. "They stopped here the day before last. Got here late. Bought a few supplies and asked for news of the latest gold strikes. Pushed on the next mornin'."

Fargo thanked him and went back out. No sooner did he step over the threshold than an arrow whizzed past his shoulder and thudded into the jamb.

4

Fargo sprang back inside, drawing his Colt as he did, and put his back to the wall.

Over at the counter Sublette was honing a skinning knife on a whetstone. "What was that sound?"

"Arrow," Fargo enlightened him, and risked a peek past the jamb.

The trading post lay in a basin about ten acres in extent. A stream meandered through it, and except where the land had been cleared for the post proper and a few small out-buildings, the basin was choked with trees and undergrowth.

Whoever had tried to kill him was well hidden.

Sublette hustled over carrying an old Hawken. He moved to the other side of the door and stared at the arrow. "That's Arapaho, unless I miss my guess."

"You don't," Fargo said. No two tribes fashioned their arrows alike. The markings, the way the arrowhead was attached, this one was Arapaho.

"I ain't got no quarrel with them," Sublette said, and gave him a pointed look.

"Me either."

"One of us is a liar," Sublette said, but he grinned as he said it. Raising his voice, he hollered in the Arapaho tongue, "This is White Hair. I am friend to the Arapaho. I trade with the Arapaho. Why do you attack my lodge?"

From out of the woods a male voice answered. "We do not attack you, White Hair. You have always been of one heart with our people."

Sublette gave a mild start. "Tall Bull? Is that you out there?"

"I and others."

The old man switched to English and said to Fargo,

"Well, now. We know it ain't me they're after. You sure you ain't got a quarrel with them? Maybe it's slipped your mind."

"Was that supposed to be funny?"

Sublette nodded at the arrow in the jamb. "Ain't nothing funny about that, sonny." He made bold to poke his head out and shout in the Arapaho tongue, "Who did you shoot at, Tall Bull?"

"The other white-eye."

Fargo had a fair idea where the warrior was but couldn't see him. Clearing his throat he shouted in the Arapaho language, "This is the other white-eye. Why do you want my life, Tall Bull?"

"You know why, killer. We found the bodies that you and your friends left to rot."

Fargo swore. The Arapahos believed that he had a hand in killing those two warriors. "Other whites were to blame. Not me. If you read the tracks you know I came along later."

"Most of the tracks were washed away by rain," Tall Bull said. "We know you spent a sleep in their camp. We know you are riding in the same direction. Why do that unless you are one of them?"

"Hell," Fargo said.

"What's this all about?" Sublette asked.

Fargo told him. As he was wrapping up his account he spied movement in the trees.

"So that's why you were askin' about them fellers who stopped here?" Sublette said. "They've put you in a tight. The Arapahos are generally peaceable but they can be downright fierce when their dander is up."

"I don't want to spill their blood if I can help it," Fargo said.

"You don't have much choice. Tall Bull is a member of their Spear Society. Do you have any notion what that means?"

Yes, Fargo did. The Spear Society was made up of the bravest warriors, all of whom swore a solemn oath to never back down to an enemy and never retreat in battle.

"I'll see what I can do for you," Sublette offered, and to Fargo's surprise, he went out. Leaning the Hawken against the wall, Sublette held his hands out from his sides. "I am unarmed, Tall Bull. I would like words with you."

"Come to us," the Arapaho yelled. "You will not be harmed. You have the word of Tall Bull."

Sublette smiled at Fargo and crossed the clearing.

Fargo hoped the old man could do some good. If he was forced to fight and any of the warriors lived to reach a village, he'd have the whole tribe out for his blood.

Sublette was gone an uncomfortably long interval.

Finally he emerged from the trees, looking troubled. Snatching his Hawken, he came back in.

"Well?" Fargo prompted when the old man just stood there.

"It doesn't look good. There's four of 'em and they're as mad as riled hornets."

"It wasn't *me*," Fargo said.

"I believe you. You have honest eyes. But Tall Bull thinks you talk with a forked tongue."

"Damn it to hell."

"There's more," Sublette said. "And it explains why he's so het up to slit your throat." The old trapper paused. "One of the two who were killed was his younger brother. They were close. Like two peas in a pod. No way he can let it pass."

Fargo swore. This had gone from bad to as worse as it could be.

"Tall Bull ain't in no frame of mind to listen to reason," Sublette went on. "He's in a blood-spillin' mood and nothin' will stop him until you've paid for his brother's life."

"What if I go out there unarmed, like you did, and talk to him?"

"You wouldn't get ten steps and you'd have more arrows in you than a porcupine has quills."

Fargo thought to ask, "Do any of them have guns?"

"Not that I saw. It's bows and lances and knives. But I wouldn't take 'em lightly."

Fargo knew better. In the hands of a seasoned warrior a bow was as lethal as a rifle. More so, since it was quieter. As for a lance, a spear through the chest or the belly was nearly always fatal.

From the woods came a shout. "White-eye! Come out and face us!"

"I'd rather they came to me," Fargo said to Sublette.

Tall Bull wasn't done. "Come out or we will set fire to

White Hair's lodge and force you to come out. We will not wait long."

The old trapper turned red in the face and stood in the doorway to holler, "How would you like it if I set fire to your lodge, Tall Bull? I am not part of this. It would be wrong of you to set fire to the post. I will not let you torch my place. Do you hear me?" He harrumphed and came back in, muttering, "I thought he claimed he was my friend."

Fargo didn't want to get Sublette in trouble with the Arapahos. It required a lot of savvy to stay friendly with the surrounding tribes in order to conduct business.

Slight just one warrior and others would take it as a sign the trader couldn't be trusted. "I won't let it come to that."

"What do you have in mind? You can't reason with them and if you try to ride off they'll shoot your horse out from under you."

That reminded Fargo. The Arapahos might take it into their heads to help themselves to the Ovaro. "I didn't ask for this," he said absently.

"That's life for you," Sublette said. "Ain't none of us asks to die, either, but the Almighty had other ideas."

"I have to go out and face them."

"You're loco."

"I'll try to take them alive if I can," Fargo said, knowing full well how foolish he sounded.

"Listen to me, son. You could be Daniel Boone, himself, and it can't be done. You try to take them breathin' and you're the one who won't be."

"Would you like it better if I stay in here until flames are licking at your roof?"

Frowning, Sublette said, "This is a hell of a note. I'm damned if you stay put and you're damned if you tangle with them."

"Don't so much as poke your head out until I let you know it's safe," Fargo cautioned and went to slip out.

Sublette grabbed his wrist. "Hold on. From what I gathered when I was talkin' to Tall Bull, there's him and another warrior out in front and warriors on both sides. I bet I could sneak you out the back and they wouldn't notice."

"There's a back door?"

"No." Sublette chuckled. "I got me a sneaky-hole that they don't know about."

"A what?"

"Had it dug back when I built the place in case hostiles ever trapped me inside." Sublette beckoned and hastened on to the counter and around to a short hall. At the other end a door opened into a storage room. Crates were stacked against a wall on one side. Attached to the other were shelves lined with trade goods.

"Come see," Sublette said, and moved to the back wall. Kneeling, he groped the logs as if feeling for something.

"These are the ones. I don't know if it will open. I haven't tried to in years."

Fargo bent closer and saw that holes had been drilled into several logs. Their purpose became clear when Sublette stuck his fingers into the holes of one of the logs, and pulled. At first nothing happened.

"Knew they would be stuck," Sublette puffed. He pulled harder. "All it should take is a little wriggling." He tugged and jerked and a two-foot length of log came loose. Grinning, he set it down, put a finger to his lips to caution silence, and peered out. "I don't see anyone," he whispered. "Help me with the others."

Three sections, in all, were removed, creating a space large enough for a man to slip through.

"You'll have to move fast," Sublette advised. "It's about ten yards to the trees."

Fargo nodded and dropped onto his hands and knees. Taking his hat off, he poked his head through. In the trees a robin warbled and nearby a yellow butterfly flitted.

The forest was deceptively peaceful. Somewhere out there, death lurked.

"What are you waitin' for?" Sublette asked.

Fargo slid out. Rising, he jammed his hat on, looked both ways, and bolted for the greenery. The nape of his neck prickled with his expectation of taking an arrow but he made it to the woods without being seen. Or so he thought as he darted around a large oak and stopped to search the vegetation for the Arapahos. He didn't have to search hard.

Not six feet away stood a startled warrior holding a lance.

5

As quick as thought the Arapaho raised his lance to hurl it.

Cursing, Fargo dived, drawing his Colt as he dropped. He swore he felt the lance brush the top of his hat and then he was on his side and the warrior was bounding at him with a knife raised to stab.

"No!" Fargo cried, but the Arapaho had bloodlust in his eyes.

Fargo fired, rolled, fired again. The warrior jerked to each impact. Scrambling, spitting blood, the Arapaho sought to bury his blade. Fargo fired a third time and the Arapaho collapsed.

Rising, Fargo glided deeper into the forest. As he ran he reloaded. The other three would be after him.

He hadn't wanted this. But now it was them or him, and he would be damned if it would be him. He came to a log and went prone on the other side. Taking off his hat, he raised his head and peered back the way he had come.

The gun blasts had silenced the birds and the squirrels and the woods were deathly quiet. So quiet Fargo could hear himself breathe.

Fargo scoured the shadows. When they came it would be swiftly and silently. He must be ready or he would be dead.

He thought of the five farmers who had brought this on his head, and he added it to the list of things they must answer for.

The branches of a small pine tree moved and a painted faced appeared. The warrior gazed about him with careful deliberation.

A second face rose out of high grass about thirty feet to the right of the first. They saw one another, and the warriors in the grass used sign language.

Fargo didn't quite catch what it was, and the next moment both faces were gone.

Fargo's skin prickled again. He hadn't spotted the third warrior yet. The man could have been anywhere, even behind him. The thought made him twist his head, and the twisting saved his life.

An arrow thudded into the log, nearly nicking his ear in its passage.

The third warrior was on his knees a stone's toss away. Whipping a hand to his quiver, he nocked another shaft and pulled the sinew string to his cheek.

Fargo shot him. He planted a slug in the center of the Arapaho's chest. The warrior thrashed violently for a bit and was still.

Grabbing his hat, Fargo jammed it on and ran. War whoops rent the woodland. An arrow flashed over his shoulder. A glance showed him that the last two were in heated pursuit, bounding like antelope.

Fargo flew around an oak. A shaft imbedded itself in the tree and then he was past and running full out. He was no city-bred gentleman with the speed of a turtle and the stamina of a newborn calf. He could run like an Apache, run for miles and not tire, and he ran now as he had seldom run, intending to put the Arapahos a good ways behind him and buy time to think. Maybe there was still a way to avoid having to kill or be killed.

But the warriors were exceptional runners, too, and their stamina wasn't a whit less than his.

Each time Fargo looked back, the pair were there. They didn't gain but they didn't lose ground, either. Soon it was apparent that fate wasn't going to let him come up with a way to spare them. It was them or him.

Fargo came to the end of the basin. Before him rose a steep incline that would take all his attention to climb and he didn't have the attention to spare. Whirling, he looked about for suitable cover but it was too late.

The Arapahos were on him.

The archer let an arrow fly. The other warrior raced at him with a lance.

Fargo twisted, and the arrow clipped a whang from his

buckskin shirt. He fired, jolting the bowman onto the heels of his moccasins. The warrior with the lance roared in outrage and his arm moved in a blur. Fargo twisted again, but he wasn't as lucky. The tip caught him on the side, tearing his buckskin shirt and ripping his flesh. It didn't stick but it hurt like hell. He brought the Colt up and shot the onrushing warrior in the face.

The bowman had vanished.

Pressing his left hand to his side, Fargo flattened and crawled. He wasn't losing much blood, thank God.

Snaking in among some cottonwoods, he sat up.

Once again quiet prevailed.

Fargo pulled up his shirt. The wound was several inches long but only about an eighth of an inch deep.

He'd been lucky. Had the lance struck a little to the left, he'd be in agony and bleeding like a stuck pig.

With a start Fargo realized he hadn't reloaded. He did so now, all too aware of how vulnerable he was. When he had six pills in the wheel he sank onto his side and crawled to the dark side of a thicket.

The minutes dragged. Fargo's side throbbed and his throat grew as dry as a desert. He began to wonder if the last warrior had given up when a silhouette reared.

The Arapaho, half-visible behind an oak, was scouring the vegetation.

Fargo stayed still.

The warrior crept into the open. He was turning his head every which way.

Curling his thumb around the Colt's hammer, Fargo waited. If the Arapaho kept coming, he would pass within a few yards of the thicket. Fargo suspected it was Tall Bull; the warrior was of uncommon height for an Arapaho, almost six and a half feet.

His bow held ready, the warrior scanned the basin's rim and then faced toward the trading post. He stopped and tilted his head. Clearly, he was perplexed. He couldn't understand where Fargo had gotten to.

Flat in the shadows, Fargo had Tall Bull dead to rights. All he had to do was squeeze the trigger. Most anyone would have. Instead, he silently rose and pointed the Colt and said quickly in Arapaho, "I did not kill your brother."

Tall Bull spun and froze on seeing the revolver. Fury animated his features.

"Did you hear me?" Fargo said.

"I heard your lie."

"It was not me."

"Perhaps not," Tall Bull snarled. "But it was one of those you were with, white-eye. And that is the same as it being you."

"I told you before," Fargo said. "I was not one of them."

"You spent the night at their camp. The signs told us that much."

"They had me tied," Fargo tried to explain. "In the morning they left me there and rode away."

Tall Bull's tone dripped sarcasm. "And you followed them to thank them?"

"Damn it," Fargo snapped, and switched to Arapaho. "I am trying not to kill you."

"As you tried not to kill my friends."

Fargo saw there was no reasoning with him. Not now. Not ever. But he tried anyway. "What will it take to make you believe me?"

"Your scalp in my lodge."

"I speak with a straight tongue," Fargo insisted.

"For killing my brother there can be no peace between us, white man," Tall Bull declared. "We are enemies forever, and for enemies there can only be death."

Fargo grasped at a straw. "What if I brought them back to you?"

"How do you mean?"

"I will bring them back alive to your village so you can deal with them as you please."

"You insult me if you think I believe you would do that."

"On my honor as a man. I will find them and force them to return whether they want to come or not."

Uncertainty etched the Arapaho's features. "You almost make me believe you."

"All I ask is that you let me try," Fargo said. "If I don't come back you can always track me down."

"How would I find you? The white world is not my world. You would be safe from my vengeance. No. You try to trick me."

"You have my promise."

"The promise of the man who killed my brother." Tall Bull grunted. "Enough talk. I will listen to no more of your lies."

"Please believe me," Fargo heard himself say.

Tall Bull's bowstring had been ever-so-slowly curving. Tall Bull tried to be clever about it but Fargo had noticed. Now, trying to distract him, Tall Bull said, "Tell me this. Why did your friends leave you?"

"They are not my friends. They are as much my enemies as they are yours."

"You are white," Tall Bull said. The implication being that white men were brothers as Arapahos were brothers.

"Do not do this," Fargo said. "I beg you."

Tall Bull looked at him, stared him straight in the eyes, and for a few seconds Fargo thought he had done it, he thought he had convinced the man to part ways in peace.

Tall Bull raised the bow, lightning fast, and pulled the string.

Fargo fired.

The slug sent Tall Bull teetering with a hole in his forehead. His fingers went limp, and the bowstring twanged.

The shaft flashed at Fargo. He felt a blow like a punch and he was jarred halfway around. Pain flooded through him. He looked at the arrow sticking from his shoulder and the blood oozing from the wound and almost passed out.

His jaw clenched rigid, Fargo staggered toward the trading post. He was halfway there when his legs gave out. He knelt there, marshaling his strength. Gripping the arrow, he yanked, but it was wedged fast.

Heaving to his feet, Fargo lurched on. He remembered a soldier who was once hit in the shoulder with an arrow, and how the tip severed sinews that never properly healed. The soldier never enjoyed the full use of his arm again.

Fargo's shoulder was wet with blood. His side was bleeding, too. He could feel the slick sensation spreading with every step.

He came to the back of the trading post and groaned when he saw that the secret hole wasn't there. The old man had stuck the logs back in.

Fargo pounded, the movement costing him precious vitality. When it was apparent the old man wasn't coming, he forced his legs to take him around the corner.

"Sublette!" he hollered, but got no answer.

With each labored breath, Fargo felt weaker. At the front he almost fell. His body refused to go on, and he had to spur it through sheer force of will.

"Sublette?" he croaked.

Fargo tottered a couple more steps. Then the world swirled, and the sky and the ground turned upside down, and he was dimly conscious of falling.

6

Fargo awoke with a start. It took him a few moments to realize where he was; on his back on a blanket on the floor of the trading post. His shirt was off, crumpled next to him. On top of it was his hat. He tried to rise onto his elbows and his right shoulder seared with agonizing fire.

The arrow had been taken out and a bandage applied. And someone was humming.

Sublette came around the counter carrying a bottle of Monongahela. "You were out about an hour," he said, hunkering.

"You doctored me?"

"Who else?" the old man said, and chuckled. Opening the bottle, he took a swig, let out a sigh of contentment, and held it out. "Care for some?"

"Does a buffalo like to roll in its own piss?" Fargo gratefully swallowed and felt life return to his limbs.

"You're a heavy coon," Sublette said. "Have a lot of muscle on you. I had to drag you in. It took some doin'." He touched the bandage. "The good Lord was watchin' over you."

"Before or after I was shot with an arrow?"

"The barb hit bone and didn't go in deep," Sublette explained. "It didn't take a lot to dig it out." He indicated Fargo's side. "That nick isn't much, either. You'll be sore for a month and then good as new."

"The Arapahos?"

Sublette frowned. "I hauled 'em off in the brush in case more come by. It'd be my hide if the rest of the tribe found out." He frowned. "I can use help with the buryin'."

"I'll do what I can," Fargo offered.

"Damned decent of you, seein' as how this is all your doin'." Sublette caught himself. "Well, those other fellers. But it was you who killed Tall Bull and his friends."

Fargo didn't care to be reminded. He sank down, feeling weak again.

"Don't let it get to you. They were out for blood." Sublette chugged from the bottle. "That arm of yours will likely be stiff for a spell. Try not to use it much for a week or so."

"I know what to do," Fargo said. He resented being treated like a greenhorn.

"Before I forget, I put your horse up out back with mine," Sublette informed him. "Even gave it a bag of oats, if that's all right."

"It's fine." Fargo was sincerely grateful.

"I reckon there's nothin' else left to do except feed you if you're hungry."

Fargo wasn't. He let the old man ramble and he drifted off. When next he awoke the chill air told him it was night. A lantern gleamed on a peg. He didn't see or hear Sublette, and remembered a door between the main room and the store room that must be where the old man slept.

Gingerly rising, he stretched his left arm but held his right pressed to his ribs.

Venturing behind the bar, Fargo helped himself to a bottle. He slapped coins on the counter to pay for it and went to a corner table. He didn't want company. He just wanted to think.

Finding the five farmers would take some doing. They had too large a lead and could have been practically anywhere. That they were bound for Rockies west of Denver didn't narrow it down much. There had been too many recent strikes.

Fargo stared at his bandaged shoulder and at the gash in his side and thought of the four dead warriors and the night he had spent trussed helpless, and he made up his mind then and there that he wouldn't rest until he caught up to them. "No matter how damn long it takes," he said out loud, and sucked down more bug juice.

A third of the bottle later he was feeling no pain. He picked up his shirt and slid into it, which was a feat in itself since he couldn't raise his right arm more than shoulder high. Every twinge reminded him of those he was hunting: Willard, Milton, Alonzo, Elias, and Rafer. He mustn't forget Rafer; that son of a bitch, in particular, had it coming.

Another third, and Fargo was ready to turn in. He made his slow way to the storage room, where he reckoned he was least likely to be disturbed, and made himself comfortable.

Holding the Colt in his hand on his chest, he wasn't long in drifting off. He didn't sleep well, though. Every now and again his shoulder spiked with torment and he'd snap awake. When he moved his arm, even a little, it felt as if tiny daggers sliced into him.

The clang of a pan roused him along about daybreak. Sitting up, he scratched and yawned and started the day with several swallows of red-eye. Stiffly rising, he discovered Sublette at the stove, putting fresh coffee on.

"There you are, sonny," the trader greeted him. "I wondered where you got to."

"I'll be leaving soon," Fargo announced.

"I figured you wouldn't waste any time, but it might be best if you stayed over one more day."

"No," Fargo said with finality.

"In my younger days I'd have done the same," Sublette said. He moved to the counter. "Did I mention that Tall Bull has a missus and three little ones?"

"Hell," Fargo said.

"Didn't mean to spoil your day," Sublette said. "Reckoned you should know, is all."

"I don't need more reasons."

Sublette nodded. "I savvy that. Between you and me, I'd hate to be in their boots when you catch up to them. Seems likely they'll be hell bound before they can blink."

Fargo was in no mood for small talk. He had coffee and a biscuit and was about to go out the door when the old man cleared his throat.

"You ain't forgettin' those bodies, are you? I meant it when I said I could use your help."

It took a lot out of him but Fargo used the Ovaro and his rope to help drag the bodies a quarter mile from the trading post. He did what little he could in digging four shallow graves.

31

"I just hope the other Arapahos don't come across these," Sublette remarked.

Fargo didn't think they would. They were well hidden.

Sublette thanked him for his help and surprised him with a bundle of food and free bottle of whiskey.

"If you're ever by this way again, stop by."

"Keep your hair," Fargo said in parting, and tapped his spurs.

His shoulder plagued him all day. Sublette had mentioned that the arrowhead nicked the bone, and Fargo figured that accounted for the persistent discomfort. Despite the pain, he was so exhausted that he got a good night's sleep under the stars.

The next morning he could raise his arm higher and move it a little more. The stiffness was going away.

The rest of his ride to Denver was uneventful. He didn't run into any hostiles or outlaws or wild beasts.

The city was thriving. Recently it had become part of the brand new Territory of Colorado and served as the hub for hordes from the East streaming to the Rockies after gold and silver. The influx had started with the Pike's Peak Gold Rush and showed no signs of abating any time soon.

There was little law and a lot of lawlessness. So many ladies of the night had taken up residence in dozens of bawdy houses that Denver, at an elevation of a mile above sea level, was jokingly referred to as the highest whorehouse in the world.

Saloons were as common as fleas on a hound dog. The city's leaders saw to it that the bawdy houses and saloons were concentrated in one area to separate the sinners from the upstanding citizens who claimed they'd never set foot in a house of ill repute.

They weren't fooling anyone.

Fargo liked the mile-high nest of vipers. It was wild and raw yet had elements of sophistication. Some of those elements were high-priced ladies who could tingle a man to his marrow.

After stabling the Ovaro, he took a small room at a boarding house, left his saddlebags and rifle on the bed, and treated himself to a shave and a bath. Soaking in a tub of hot water did wonders for his shoulder.

His next order of business was to fill his belly. At a fancy restaurant with napkins on every table and high-backed chairs with soft seats, he ordered beefsteak with all the trimmings. He wasn't disappointed. The steak was an inch and a half thick and dripped bloody juice. A heaping helping of potatoes smeared in butter, a generous portion of green beans and carrots, and warm slices of bread completed the meal. He washed it all down with six cups of scalding coffee. When he was done he sat back and patted his belly. The waiter asked if he wanted dessert and Fargo treated himself to apple pie.

Feeling like a whole new man, Fargo strolled out into the cool of the evening. He aimed to have some fun and at the same time ask around about the five farmers. It was a needle in a haystack, given that Denver's population was reputed to be all of four thousand people, but there was always a chance.

The air was crisp. Even though it was summer, several of the peaks to the west were capped by snowy mantles.

Fargo was strolling along drinking in the sights when a young woman in a tight pink and green dress came sashaying toward him twirling a parasol. Luxurious black curls cascaded past her slender shoulders. She had eyes as blue as his own, and a figure that would make an hourglass green with envy.

Brazenly stopping in front of him and looking him up and down, she grinned and said, "Well, what do we have here?"

"A horny son of a bitch," Fargo said.

She laughed merrily. "And you're clean and smell of lilac water, too."

"You have a good nose."

Jiggling her bosom, she grinned and said, "Is that all you've noticed?"

Fargo nodded. "I'm a nose man."

Another gay laugh tinkled from the woman's smooth throat. Placing a small hand on his wrist, she leaned close and breathed in his ear, "How do you do, handsome? I'm Elizabeth. All my friends call me Beth. All my really good friends call me easy."

Fargo chuckled and playfully smacked her bottom. "You are just what I've been looking for."

"The most talented tart this side of anywhere?"

"A female."

Beth squeezed his wrist and brushed her hip against his. "I like a man who makes me smile."

"How do you feel about a man who makes you gush?"

Her smile was lascivious. "I like them even more."

"My place or yours?"

"Does yours have a four-poster bed big enough for the queen of England?" Beth asked, and when he shook his head, she said, "Then my place it is. I'll even treat you to drinks and all the small talk you want."

"To hell with that," Fargo said. "I just want to screw you silly."

7

It was called the Lavender House. It sat on the corner of Fremont and Beeker Streets, on a hill that overlooked much of the city. Three stories high, it had gables and arches and a wide porch that ran completely around the bottom floor. Out back was an area for carriages and buggies to park.

The clientele included a lot of the well-to-do and city officials. Beth boasted of that as they climbed the steps to the porch.

Men in bowlers and derbies and suits were huddled with women in colorful dresses.

Fargo's buckskins attracted attention. He ignored the stares as Beth led him through double glass doors and across a carpeted foyer to wide stairs. Mahogany walls gleamed with polish and a chandelier sparkled.

"Not bad," Fargo commented.

"It's the best house in Denver," Beth said. "Madam Currier doesn't mistreat her girls, like a lot of madams do. She knows the business inside out and she has important connections. I can't tell you how happy I was when she chose me to be part of her stable."

"Giddyup."

"I mean it," Beth said as they came to a landing and walked along a hall with more plush carpet. "You have no notion what it's like for a girl working her way up. The beatings. The abuse. And worse." She smiled and ran her hand along the wall. "I love it here. It's the nicest place I've ever worked. I hope I can stay until I'm too old and ugly for anyone to want me."

"That'll be the day."

Beth stopped and smiled and kissed him on the lips. "What a sweet thing to say. I think I like you."

Pulling her to him, Fargo kissed her long and hungrily. When he broke the kiss he said, "You think?"

"Hey, this is a business. Some of the customers I like. Some I don't but I do them anyway because that's what they pay me for."

"Any gent who would mistreat you is a jackass."

Beth pulled him to a door. "Oh, it's not that so much. I have this peeve. A lot of men don't hardly ever wash. Even important men like senators and bankers. Then their teeth are stained from all that tobacco they chew. And some have breath that would gag a mule."

"I don't chew," Fargo said.

Beth opened the door and moved aside for him to enter first. "I noticed that about you right away. Like I said, you're clean and handsome and you have a sense of humor. What more can a lady ask for?"

"A hard one?"

Beth burst into peals of mirth and pecked him on the neck. "God, you make me laugh."

Her room was as lavishly furnished as the rest of the house. She hadn't been joking about the four-poster. It was wide enough to sleep seven and so soft that when Fargo sat on the edge, he sank six inches.

"Nice."

"I told you." Beth knelt. Gripping his left boot, she tugged and twisted.

"We can always do it with my boots on," Fargo said.

"Like hell. Those spurs of yours would rip the quilt to shreds." Beth grunted and jerked and his boot came off. Setting it down toes-in under the bed, she gripped the other. "Any special way you like it? I can have some marmalade or whipped cream brought up."

"Hellfire," Fargo said. "Your body is enough."

"You should see some of the things other men like. One squirts lemon juice on me and licks it off."

"Lemon juice?" Fargo said, and laughed.

"Another customer is into whips. And there's a Southerner who likes to get on my back and ride me like a horse."

Fargo was tired of hearing about her clients. His right

36

boot came off, and he bent and pulled her onto his lap and nuzzled her cleavage. She smelled of perfume and powder.

"So there's nothing at all special you'd care for?" Beth persisted.

"You," Fargo said. "Naked."

"I aim to please, kind sir." Grinning, Beth removed her hat and tossed it aside.

Fargo helped with the rest. She didn't have a lot of buttons and stays but her shoes were a bitch to get off. Under her tight dress was a white cotton chemise but not any petticoats. Her stockings were white, with white garters.

Placing her on her back, Fargo crooked her left leg and peeled the stocking from her thigh to her toes. Her thighs smelled of perfume, too. He licked one and ran his hand up the other and she wriggled and giggled.

"I like playful men."

Fargo finished undressing her and she sank down with her head on a pillow and enticingly arched her back so her breasts jutted, while suggestively moving her legs.

No doubt about it, she was exquisite. From the halo of shiny hair to her upthrust nipples to the flat of her belly and the fullness of her thigh, she was enough to bring a lump of raw desire to a man's throat. She sure as hell did to his.

"Like what you see, handsome?"

"I like," Fargo admitted. He stripped off his shirt and his pants and even removed his ankle sheath, and climbed on the bed beside her. Stretching on his side, he kissed her mouth and her ear and her throat.

Beth ran her hands down his broad back and around to his gut. "You have more muscles than most."

"I have this muscle," Fargo said, and taking her hand, he placed it on his pole.

"Oh my," Beth breathed, looking down. "I have found a redwood." She grinned and winked and bent.

The lump in Fargo's throat grew bigger. So did his manhood. He took it as long as he could without exploding, then raised her off and molded his mouth to hers. Her lips were silken, her tongue a wet dervish. She kissed passionately, or pretended to. He sculpted her shoulders and caressed lower until he cupped both breasts. Her nipples were tacks. He pinched one and then the other and both at the same time, and she cooed and ground against him.

"Yes," she said. "Yes."

Fargo bent his mouth to a melon. He nipped and flicked and rimmed the nipple with his tongue while squeezing the other. Her breasts swelled.

For her part, Beth's hands were everywhere that she could reach, exploring, kneading. Her leg rubbed his. Her nether mount pressed his manhood.

Fargo licked her rippling stomach, stuck his tongue into her navel. When he eased lower, she gasped. Her thighs clamped and she pressed on his head and gave out loud moans of pure pleasure.

"That's it. Just like that. Oh, God. You're great. You're more than great."

Some men liked prattle. Fargo wasn't one of them. But he was too preoccupied to say anything and she went on praising and groaning and thrusting until all of a sudden she gushed. It seemed to catch her by surprise. Her body became a bow and she moaned louder than ever and whined and her body went into the rapturous convulsions of release. When she was done she lay spent and smiling in contentment.

Fargo straightened and slid his legs between hers. She automatically parted them, and looked into his eyes.

"You're magnificent."

Gripping his member, Fargo slid it up and down her slit a few times.

Beth shivered and dug her nails into his shoulder.

"I'm serious," she said softly into his ear. "You won't believe me but I don't say that to many."

Fargo inserted the tip and poised on his hands. He kissed her on the mouth, and it was as if she tried to devour him.

Levering on his legs, Fargo impaled her. Her eyes opened wide and her mouth parted and she uttered a tiny cry. Her legs rose to clamp around his waist.

"Oh God," Beth mewed.

Fargo rocked, her sheath a perfect fit for his saber, her inner walls clinging tight. In and out, in and out, in rising tempo. The four-poster bounced under them, the canopy rustled over their heads.

Beth's eyelids fluttered and her hips rose and she gushed anew, slamming into him as if fit to break him in half.

Fargo matched her carnal ferocity. He rammed and rammed and felt his own release build until there was no holding back even if he wanted to. The floodgates burst, and for a short span he forgot all about what brought him to Denver.

Afterward, she and he napped, Beth's cheek on his chest, her arm over his shoulder. Her breath fluttered on his neck.

When Fargo woke the window was in shadow and the room almost dark. His shoulder was hurting. He flexed his arm, then eased out from under Beth and got dressed. As he was pulling on his last boot she stirred and rolled onto her back and lay looking at him through sleepy, sultry eyes.

"Did I say you were magnificent?"

"You're not bad yourself."

"If by not bad you mean terrific I will take that as a compliment." She grinned and entwined her fingers behind her head. "God, I wish I could spend the rest of the night with you."

Fargo stomped his boot to settle it on his foot. "Heard about any new gold strikes?"

Beth gave him a puzzled look. "You sure don't strike me as a prospector."

"I'm looking for some men who are looking to get rich quick," Fargo explained.

"Friends of yours?"

"Not exactly."

"Oh." Beth propped herself on a couple of pillows. Her hair fell to above her nipples and she idly curled it with her fingers as she talked. "Let's see now. There's Pike's Peak but that's old news. There have been strikes along the South Platte and Clear Creek." She pondered a minute and said, "These gents you're after, do they know anything about how to find ore or pan a stream?"

"I doubt it."

"Then Tarryall might be your best bet. Someone found gold on Tarryall Creek a while back and a town sprang up.

Then just a couple of weeks ago there was a new find on Crooked Creek, which feeds into Tarryall." Beth laughed. "There was the usual nonsense about how nuggets were lying on the ground waiting to be plucked. If these men you're after are new here, that's where they're liable to head."

"I'm obliged," Fargo said. It sounded like something that would appeal to Willard and company.

"If you go up there, watch out," Beth warned. "Tarryall is as wild and woolly as they come. It's said someone is planted on Boot Hill practically every night."

"I don't aim to be one of them."

"We never know, do we?" Beth said.

8

To reach the boomtown, Fargo had to do a lot of riding and a lot of climbing. Tarryall was high on a tableland known as South Park. Covering over a thousand square miles, the region was remote, and dangerous. Grizzlies and mountain lions were common. The Utes were around, and they took a dim view of white men helping themselves to land the Utes had roamed for as long as any Ute could remember.

Tarryall had sprung up at the junction of North and Middle Tarryall Creeks. From its start the town had a bad reputation. Greed was the dominating passion. A parson was famous for sermonizing that it had more sinners per block than Denver, which took some doing. It had more shootings and knifings, too.

Tarryall was so wicked that law-abiding folks started a town of their own a short distance away and gave it the name Fairplay.

It had been no idle warning on Beth's part for Fargo to watch himself. He was taking his life into his hands going there. But that was fine by him. He did the same every day in the wilds.

Tarryall was nearly two miles above sea level. A high pass had to be crossed to reach the tableland, and Fargo found himself trailing a supply train of half a dozen wagons on the morning he reached it. He caught up to the lead wagon and rode beside it as they started over.

The driver was a crusty coot with a bulge in his cheek from a wad of tobacco. He constantly chewed and spat and talked to his mules, which plodded along paying him no mind. After a couple of minutes of furtive glances, he finally looked directly at Fargo and said, "Nice day, Mary Jane."

Fargo snorted.

"You like ridin' in my shade, or what?"

"Make this run regular, do you?" Fargo asked.

"Maybe I do and maybe I don't," the driver said. "What's it to you?"

"Are you always this friendly?" Fargo rejoined.

"Nah. This is my good mood. When I'm grumpy I spit on those who annoy me."

"You're welcome to spit on me," Fargo said.

The driver's eyes narrowed suspiciously. "I am?"

Fargo nodded. "So long as you don't mind me shooting you in your goddamned mouth."

Cackling in delight, the driver slapped his leg. "Didn't take you for no choir boy," he said by way of praise. "My handle is Chaw, by the way."

"Wonder how you got that," Fargo said drily.

Chaw spat over the other side and wiped his mouth with his stained sleeve. "What can I do for you?"

"I'm looking for five jackasses . . ."

"The real kind or those with two legs?" Chaw interrupted, and chortled.

"They have two legs," Fargo said.

"Ever been to Tarryall?"

"If I had, we wouldn't be having this talk."

"Ah. Well." Chaw scratched his stubble and his brow furrowed. "Let's see. There's the Stopover. Has cots for a couple of bits a night. Pretty popular with those just in and headin' for the diggin's. Run by a right pretty gal, too. Name of Marian. Like in that story about the fella with the bow."

"The bow?" Fargo said.

"You know. He ran around in green long johns. Robbed from those as have to give to those as have not."

Fargo had to think before it came to him. "Robin Hood?"

"That's the one. She's about the best lookin' gal in town but you don't want to let on that she is or she's liable to bust your skull."

"Interesting," Fargo said.

"It's your funeral. But that's where I'd start my hunt were I you."

"Anywhere else?"

"The Emporium on Spruce Street. It's where most go to outfit. But the owner's not likely to recollect five out of the hundreds that go through every week."

"That many?"

"Hell, that's on slow weeks," Chaw said. He spat and wiped his mouth. "Watch your back. There ain't never been a town like Tarryall. I thought I'd seen it all but I hadn't come close. It's the god-awfulest nest of sidewinders on earth."

"You make it up there and back all right."

"They need to eat, the same as anybody," Chaw said. "They ain't about to make us freighters mad or they'd starve."

"I'm obliged," Fargo said, and lifted his reins to ride on ahead.

"One thing," Chaw said quickly.

"I'm listening," Fargo responded when the man didn't go on.

"You fight shy of Bully Bob. Salty as you are, he's got a dozen gun sharks in his pay and he likes to let them sink their teeth in."

"That's his name? Bully Bob?"

"No, it's Robert. Robert Shanks. He's from Illinois or some such. Everyone calls him Bully Bob behind his back on account of that's what he is. He's the cock of the roost and that's no lie."

"What about the law?"

"In Tarryall?" Chaw said, and laughed. "Mister, the only law in that pit of iniquity is be quick or be dead. They've got a marshal over to Fairplay but his tin ends at the town limits."

"And people put up with it."

"Who's to object? The few decent folks who have stayed don't dare speak up or they'll lose their teeth, or worse."

"I'm obliged," Fargo said again.

"Wait," Chaw said. "Be nice to know who I've been jawin' with."

Fargo told him.

Chaw stopped chewing. He glanced at Fargo's Colt and at Fargo's face and said, "Heard of you."

"Have you, now?"

"I've been around a good long while and I have good

ears," Chaw said. He grinned. "Land sakes. Here I've been talkin' to someone famous and didn't know it."

"Those damn newspapers."

Chaw spat but didn't wipe his mouth. "Them, and folks naturally love to gossip. You don't want to be gabbed about, you shouldn't go around killin' so many folks."

"Hell," Fargo said.

"I'm just sayin'," Chaw said. "Me, I'm keepin' my ears peeled. A gent like you loose in Tarryall, there should be a heap of new gossip before too long."

"I'm not looking for trouble."

"No, just five jackasses, as you called 'em." Chaw squinted at him. "What do you aim to do once you find 'em?"

Fargo didn't answer.

Chaw nodded. "I thought so. Well, there's plenty of space left on Boot Hill."

About to gig the Ovaro, Fargo thought to say, "I'd appreciate it if you kept our talk to yourself."

"My lips are sealed," Chaw said.

Fargo rode on, frowning. He'd be willing to bet that before the week was out, everyone in Tarryall would know he was there and that he was looking for five men. He put it from his mind and concentrated on his riding.

Once over the pass, the road wound down through heavy timber to miles and miles of grassy tableland. Tarryall was near a series of hills, with snow-clad mountains as a backdrop.

It turned out that Fargo had been misinformed. There was Tarryall: bawdy, gaudy, and with an unequalled reputation for villainy. There was Fairplay: a few miles away over Red Hill, it was devout, quiet, and pious.

And there was a third town.

Called Hamilton after the man who founded it, its citizenry was made up of malcontents who didn't much care for Tarryall's larcenous ways but were too lazy to move as far as Fairplay so they just walked across the creek and started a new town. Now Tarryall and Hamilton were bitter rivals for government favors and in fleecing the gold-hungry hordes.

To Fargo it was all perfectly ridiculous, but then, so was a lot of what passed for civilization. He entered Tarryall at one end of the main street and promptly drew rein in amazement. In his wide-flung wanderings he'd seen a lot of boomtowns but never any like this.

Tarryall pulsed with life and noise. Every street, every boardwalk, was crammed with people. Every hitch rail was lined with horses. From dozens of saloons came the hubbub of voices mixed with coarse laughter and the tinny notes of misplayed pianos. Occasionally a shot rang out but everyone went on with whatever they were doing.

Sprawled around the business district were some three hundred log cabins and other dwellings. In a testament to optimism, there was also a church.

The finest building in the whole town was the Dunbar House, an expensive hotel. Tarryall also had the distinction of its own private mint. There was talk that the federal government was going to make private mints illegal but they hadn't gotten around to it yet.

Fargo rode down the main street looking for an empty space to tie off the Ovaro. As luck would have it, a bedraggled lump of a drunk stumbled out of a saloon called the Lucky Lady, climbed on a swayback, and headed for God-knew-where. Fargo quickly reined over and dismounted. He debated whether to take the Henry or leave it in the scabbard; he didn't want it stolen. Others had left their rifles in their scabbards so he figured it was safe enough and went to the batwings.

Noise and odors washed over him. The place was packed. Every chair at every table was filled. The bar was elbows from end to end.

Fargo pushed on the batwings and strode in. He shouldered through the press to the near end of the bar and thumped it to get the bartender's attention. He ordered a whiskey to wash down the dust and when the glass was set in front of him and the man was pouring, he asked, "Where do I find the Stopover?"

"Down two blocks and turn left. But I hear they are full up."

Fargo paid and turned and leaned back with the drink in his hand. He raised the glass to his lips, and froze.

Not twenty feet away, seated at a table playing poker, was

45

Rafer. He had a half-empty bottle beside him, and his rifle was across his lap.

"Well, well," Fargo said to himself. He drained the redeye with a gulp, smacked the glass down, and circled until he was a few feet from his quarry.

Rafer was intent on his cards. He was gnawing his lower lip and fingering the few coins he had left.

"You in or not, mister?" another player demanded.

"I reckon so." Rafer pushed his coins into the pot and glanced up and saw Fargo. He turned to stone.

"Why did you stop?" the same man asked, and he and the rest looked up.

Fargo planted himself, his right thumb hooked in his gun belt only an inch from his Colt. "Anyone who doesn't want to catch lead by mistake had best move."

9

Four chairs emptied so fast, the men in them nearly tripped over their own feet.

Rafer placed his hands on the edge of the table above his rifle. "Look who it is," he said with a scowl. "Didn't ever figure to set eyes on you again."

"Small world," Fargo said.

The sudden scrambling and pushing had caused a dozen or more people to stop what they were doing and stare. Those nearest Fargo edged away from him. Those behind Rafer did the same.

"You came all this way just for us?" Rafer asked.

"Where are your pards?"

"I'll be damned." Rafer grinned and ran a finger along the table's rim. "You must hate us a powerful lot to go to this much bother."

"Where?"

Rafer placed his hand flat and sat back. "What are your intentions?"

"You tied me and beat me and left me to die," Fargo said. "What the hell do you think my intentions are?"

"We left you breathin'," Rafer amended. "Not that I wanted to but it should count for somethin'."

"It doesn't," Fargo said.

"Got a lot of bark on you," Rafer said. "But I'm not about to say where they are, not even if you try to beat it out of me."

"Then I guess we're done talking."

Rafer nodded. "I'm goin' to enjoy this. I hate Injun lovers as much as I hate anything."

"I hate stupid," Fargo said.

"Do you know what your problem is? You're too cocksure of yourself. You don't know how to bend with the wind."

"Mister, you don't know a damn thing about me."

"I know enough." Rafer sighed. "But fine. We'll do this your way. And when I've blown you to hell, say howdy to those two Injun friends of yours."

"I never met them," Fargo said.

"You will," Rafer returned, and speared his hands for the Spencer. He almost had it above the table when Fargo's first slug slammed into his chest and rocked his chair. He jerked the Spencer higher and pointed the muzzle as the second shot tore into his throat. His head snapped back and he screeched like a gut-shot lynx and again tried to shoot.

Fargo fanned a shot into his forehead. The Spencer clattered to the floor and Rafer melted from his chair into a scarlet-flecked pile of disjointed limbs.

The Lucky Lady had gone completely silent. Not so much as a glass tinkled. All eyes were on the dead man on the floor.

Fargo reloaded and twirled the Colt into his holster. He walked over, picked up the Spencer, and set it on the table.

Whispers and murmuring broke out. Men and doves pointed.

A man with sickle-shaped side whiskers, wearing a brown suit, bustled out of the back and stood with his hands on his hips, glowering. "What in hell do you think you're doing?"

"Leaving," Fargo said.

"Like hell you are. I'm Jack Wayne. The owner. Look at what you've done."

"He went for his gun first."

"I don't mean that." Wayne nodded at the body. "Look at the blood he's leaking. It's all over my damn floor."

Fargo stared at the slowly spreading red pool. "That happens when you put bullet holes in somebody."

"Are you trying to be funny?" Wayne said. "Because I don't find it funny at all. Grab a bucket and mop and clean this mess up."

Fargo faced him. "That's what you have hired help for."

"No," Wayne said angrily. "I have help to tend bar and

sweep out the place and empty the spittoons after we close for the night. I don't hire anyone to clean up blood."

Fargo forked a finger in his pocket and produced a double eagle. "This should more than cover it."

Wayne made no move to take the coin. "You're not listening. *You* made the mess. *You* clean it up."

"This is a first," Fargo said. He'd been involved in more than a few saloon shootings and no one ever brought up cleaning the mess.

Wayne pointed at a man in an apron. "Harvey, fetch a bucket and a mop."

"Yes, sir, boss, right away."

"Give Harvey this and have him do it," Fargo said, and flipped the coin at Wayne.

The saloon owner caught it and made as if to throw it back. "You're not listening. It's not Harvey's job. It's not the bartender's. It's yours."

Fargo turned to go.

Jack Wayne moved to block his way. "Hold on, damn you. Try walking out and so help me I'll get word to Robert Shanks."

Fargo paused.

"Heard of him, have you?" Wayne said smugly. "I pay him for protection. All I have to do is snap my fingers and he'll send some of his gun hands to deal with you."

"He protects you from blood on your floor?"

"You know what I mean," Jack Wayne said curtly. "What will it be? Clean up the mess you made or have Mr. Shanks send his curly wolves?"

"Send them," Fargo said.

"Are you hankering to die? Is that it? Because Robert Shanks will sure as hell oblige you."

Fargo made for the batwings. Everyone was staring at him as if they expected him to be shot dead any second. He was about to push on out when a metallic click from behind stopped him in his tracks.

"You're not going anywhere," Jack Wayne said.

The bartender was holding a cocked double-barreled shotgun pointed at Fargo.

Just then Harvey hurried back with the bucket and mop. He set the bucket next to Jack Wayne and placed the mop in it. "Here you go, boss."

"What the hell are you giving them to me for, you idiot?" Wayne snapped, and jabbed a thumb at Fargo. "Give them to him."

"And no funny moves," the bartender warned, hefting the shotgun, "or I'll blow you in half."

At that, everyone within twenty feet of Fargo anxiously backed away.

Harvey brought the bucket and mop and placed them at Fargo's feet. "Sorry mister," he said so only Fargo could hear. "I'm just doin' as the boss says." He hastened out of howitzer range.

"I'm waiting," Wayne said imperiously.

Fargo stared into the twin muzzles of the shotgun. He knew he could draw and put a slug between the bartender's eyes before the man could blink, but in reflex the bartender's trigger finger might close on those twin triggers and pieces of him would be all over the walls, ceiling, and floor. He slowly went to reach for the mop.

Unexpectedly, an older man stepped from between the press of patrons around the bartender. He wore an old army uniform, faded and rough from too much wear, and torn in spots. He had gray hair and gray eyes and gray stubble. He wore a Remington with walnut grips, and as he came forward he drew it and cocked it and jammed it against the bartender's head. "You splatter him, mister, and I splatter your brains."

The bartender stiffened.

"I'll be damned," Fargo said.

The gray man smiled. "Fancy seeing you again, hoss. It's been a spell," he said. "Too damn long."

"That it has, Mac," Fargo replied fondly. Jim McCullock had been an army quartermaster and a friend. They'd shared more bottles of whiskey than there were days in the year. One day McCullock had announced he was getting too old to be getting up at the crack of dawn and marching on parade and had gone off, as McCullock put it, to sit in the sun and take the rest of his days easy.

Apparently Jack Wayne knew the old scout, too. "What the hell is this, Mac?"

"You see me with my pistol to this fella's head," Mc-Cullock said. "It's not plain enough for you?"

Wayne bobbed a chin at Fargo. "Is this hombre a friend of yours?"

"One of the best," McCullock said, "and I'd be obliged if this tub would let down those hammers and give me his cannon and go back to spilling bug juice."

"You shouldn't butt in," Wayne said.

McCullock shrugged. "What are friends for if not backing a friend when he needs a hand?"

"I won't forget this," Wayne growled.

"I'm too old and ornery to scare, Jack," McCullock said. "Can we get this over with before I get any older? Tubby, here, is quaking like pudding. He's making me nervous."

"Put down the shotgun, Tom," Wayne said.

The bartender was only too happy to comply and raised his arms. "There you go. Just like you told me to."

McCullock set the shotgun on the floor, stepped over it, and came to Fargo's side. Facing the room, he kept his Remington trained on Wayne. "Don't be mad now, Jack. I'm only doing what you'd do if you were in my boots."

"Mr. Shanks will hear of this."

"That's your answer to everything," McCullock said. "Run to him like he's your ma. You should grow a pair some day."

"That mouth of yours," Wayne said.

McCullock grinned at Fargo. "How about we take a stroll? This place is too stuffy."

His hand on his Colt, Fargo backed to the batwings. "Let it drop," he said to Wayne.

"That will be the day."

Fargo went through the batwings first and Jim McCullock followed. The moment they were outside, they turned and went half a block and stood and waited to see if Wayne would send someone after them but no one came out of the Lucky Lady.

McCullock chuckled and clapped Fargo on the arm. "Like old times, eh?"

Fargo held out his hand. "It's good to see you again, Mac."

The former quartermaster shook. "And you're sure a sight for this old buzzard's tired eyes."

"You can hold your own with men half your age," Fargo said.

"Used to, I could." McCullock sighed and holstered the Remington. "I meant what I said. I'm glad as glad can be to see you again."

Fargo grinned. "Gone mushy in your old age, have you?"

"Yes, sir," McCullock said. "You don't know it but you're the answer to my prayers."

10

Jim McCullock said he had a place where he was staying and invited Fargo for a drink.

Fargo accepted, but first he collected the Ovaro. He kept an eye on the batwings of the Lucky Lady while doing so.

"One thing," McCullock said as they turned down a side street. "Jack Wayne likely will get word to Robert Shanks, who is pretty much top dog in Tarryall—"

"So I keep hearing," Fargo said.

"—and he keeps a tight rein on things. Most of the killing and robbing hereabouts is his doing." McCullock rubbed his chin. "I've had a run-in with him my own self, sad to say."

"Oh?"

"Some of his hired help got in my face."

"And you showed them that was a mistake," Fargo guessed.

McCullock smiled. "I keep telling you I ain't as spry as I used to be."

They turned down a second, narrower, street, and in a few blocks turned into yet a third. Barely wide enough for a buckboard, it was lined by small cabins and shacks. A woman in homespun was doing wash in a tub, her arms in water up to her elbows. Her children were shucking corn. An elderly couple in tattered clothes sat in rocking chairs in front of a cabin that needed chinking and could use glass in the windows.

"The poor part of town," McCullock said. He went a little farther and turned in. A pitiful excuse for a fence enclosed a mostly dirt yard. There was no gate. They walked up to a shack that was one of the shabbiest on the whole street.

"This is yours?" Fargo said in some surprise.

"I pay rent," McCullock said.

"Who owns it?" Fargo asked, and by the expression that

came over his friend, he answered his own question with, "Don't tell me. Robert Shanks."

"He owns a lot and has his fingers in a lot more that he doesn't," McCullock said. He climbed a pair of cracked planks that served for steps. "Here. Let me get us a bottle and we'll sit and jaw a spell."

The chair didn't appear strong enough to bear the weight of a flea so Fargo sat on the edge of the narrow porch, which consisted of a warped piece of wood, and rested his arms on his knees.

McCullock came out with two glasses and a bottle about a third full. He sat next to Fargo and filled a glass halfway. "This one is yours."

Fargo looked at the shack and the few clumps of grass in the yard. "I seem to recollect you had a nest egg saved up."

The old quartermaster winced as if he'd been struck. "I did. I figured to find me a nice place somewhere and take it easy. I could have lived modest on what I'd saved."

"But?"

Taking a swallow, McCullock swirled what was left in his glass, and frowned. "But modest wasn't enough. I tried, Skye. I truly did. I went to Missouri and bought me a little house in Springfield and aimed to spend the rest of my days growing older."

"But?" Fargo said again when he didn't go on.

"But it was boring as hell." McCullock bowed his head. "I missed army life. Didn't think I would but I do. We miss the things we're used to, I guess." He looked up. "You know how it is."

Fargo nodded.

"I took it into my head that I wasn't going to sit in no damn rocking chair for the rest of my days. I sold my house and came west again, not really knowing what I would do. Spent about six months in Denver trying to make up my mind. Then I heard about the gold strike up this way, and figured I'd try my hand."

"You didn't."

"I know, I know," McCullock said, sounding embarrassed. "You'd think I'm old enough to know better. But I thought if I could add to my nest egg, I'd have enough to travel. To see the world, as folks say. I've always had a hankering to visit Paris and see those ladies with hair under their arms, and that other place with the big clock—"

"London."

"That's the one."

"But to go after gold," Fargo said.

"I played it smart, or thought I did. I rode all over and finally staked a claim on Crooked Creek."

"That's where they've had the latest strike," Fargo recollected.

McCullock nodded. "It's up on the north side of Little Baldy Mountain. I used nearly all the money I had to buy my claim."

"Have you found any gold?"

Before the old quartermaster could answer, two men turned into the yard. Both were tall and lean and wore tied-down six-shooters. The man on the right was the better dresser, with a black jacket and a black hat and a black leather gun belt with silver conchos. The other man wore scruffier clothes and hadn't shaved in a week and had a narrow face and dark ferret eyes.

"Uh-oh," McCullock said quietly. "I wasn't expecting them so soon."

"Who are they?" Fargo asked.

The two men stopped and the man in the black hat and jacket nodded at McCullock. "He sent us to see if you've made up your mind yet."

The other man snickered and said with a Southern drawl, "You better have, you old coot."

"Who are they?" Fargo asked again.

"I'll explain in a bit," McCullock answered, and turned to his visitors. "No need for me to make up my mind when I've already told you the answer is no."

The scruffy man bristled and said, "He'd like for you to change your thinkin'. Didn't we make that clear the last time?"

"It's still no," McCullock said.

"He won't like that," the scruffy one said. "He won't like that at all."

"I filed on it. I'll keep it."

"You'll wish you hadn't," the scruffy one said. "I have half a mind to pistol-whip you."

The man in the black hat was studying Fargo. "Behave yourself, Jareck. We don't do anything without orders. All we're to do now is ask, polite-like, if he's come to his senses."

"You know the boss will send us back here, Clyburn," Jareck said. "You know he'll want us to persuade this mule head."

"Not now, not ever," McCullock told him. "You can tell your boss to go to hell."

Jareck bristled and took a step but Clyburn put a restraining hand on his arm.

"I won't tell you twice to tone down that temper of yours."

Jareck opened his mouth as if to argue but closed it again, and nodded. "Whatever you say."

That told Fargo that Clyburn not only favored better clothes, he was the smarter of the pair, and the more dangerous.

Clyburn smiled at McCullock. "Just so we're clear. You really want me to tell Mr. Shanks that you said he can go to Hades?"

At last Fargo understood. Stretching his legs, he leaned back on his elbows and rested his right hand on his Colt.

The man called Clyburn noticed, and grinned.

"Tell him whatever you like," McCullock was saying. "It's my claim and it'll stay my claim."

"You're a jackass, old man," Jareck spat. "How many times have you gone up there and not found enough to fill a poke? Mr. Shanks is offerin' you a fair price."

"Half of what I paid isn't my idea of fair."

"It is when you don't have all that much to show for all your pannin' and diggin'."

"It's there. I've seen plenty of color. Now go away, you nuisance," McCullock said.

"When I'm damn good and ready."

Fargo decided enough was enough. "You're ready now," he said.

Jareck gave him a look of contempt. "Who the hell are you?"

"He's a friend of mine," McCullock said. "Leave him out of this."

"He shouldn't open his mouth, then," Jareck remarked.

"I've never been in a town where so many people are so stupid," Fargo said.

Clyburn chuckled.

"What the hell is so funny?" Jareck said. "He just called me brainless."

"You are," Clyburn said.

"I maybe can't read like you can or use some of the fancy words you do but I ain't stupid," Jareck said sulkily. Wheeling on his boot heels, he stalked off, his spurs jangling.

Clyburn turned to McCullock. "He'll make it worse for you with Shanks. He doesn't have much between his ears but he's a damn good hater." Clyburn started to turn and looked at Fargo. "Didn't catch your name."

"Didn't give it."

Clyburn stood there for all of ten seconds, and smiled. "If you stick around we'll find out sooner or later."

"Later then," Fargo said.

Jareck was waiting out by the street and when Clyburn joined him the pair strolled off.

"They are mighty slick with their hardware," McCullock commented. "Two of Shanks's best shooters."

"When did he offer to buy you out?"

"Three days ago. From what I hear, he's buyin' up all he can along Crooked Creek. That's his way. He waits for others to find gold, then buys up all the claims and reaps the rewards."

"I can't wait to meet him."

"Yes, you can," McCullock said. "He's a mean one. He's always all smiles and claps you on the back and calls you his friend, but under that smile is a rabid timber wolf."

"I've met his kind before."

McCullock was quiet a bit and then said, "I'm damn glad I ran into you."

To lighten his spirits, Fargo nudged him and said, "Who do I have to kill to get some food around here?"

"I'll treat you," McCullock said, standing. "I know a food trough that's cheap but the food is good."

"You're not worried about running into Shanks?"

"He won't have me gunned down in broad daylight. That's not his style. He sends his gunnies in the night to do his dirty work." McCullock beamed and smacked him on the shoulder. "Trust me. We don't have a thing to worry about."

11

After Fargo had stripped the Ovaro and placed his saddle-bags and saddle and the Henry in McCullock's shack, they bent their steps into town.

The old quartermaster gave Fargo a tour of the high points, pointing out the only saloon that didn't water its whiskey and another where the doves were uncommonly pretty.

"And that there," McCullock said as they came up to a long, low building set a little ways back from the street, "is the place you were asking me about."

The Stopover wasn't much to look at outside but inside it was clean and warm. The main room was lined with cots in orderly rows. At that time of day few were occupied. There was a small office at the front and a woman was at a desk writing in a ledger.

Fargo went in, and stopped short. That freight driver, Chaw, hadn't exaggerated when he mentioned that the owner was pretty. She was more than pretty. She was beautiful.

Her hair was an unusual reddish-yellow that shimmered in the sunlight streaming in the window. Her face was the kind a man could stare at all day and not tire looking at: oval, with a slight upturn to her button nose, and lips as ripe as plump cherries. Her dress was simple yet on her seemed elegant. Her figure, from what Fargo could tell with her in a chair, was another sight a man would never tire of admiring.

She must have sensed he was there because she suddenly looked up. Vivid blue eyes fixed on him with startling intensity and she said in a voice that had a husky tinge, "May I help you?"

"Are you Marian?" Fargo asked.

"I am." She smiled, and her teeth were as perfect as the rest of her.

Fargo doffed his hat and went to the desk. "I'm looking for four men. Well, there were five. Farmers from Kansas. It could be they've taken cots for the night the past couple of days."

"I can't help you," she said, and bent to the ledger.

"You didn't even think about it," Fargo said.

Marian wrote while saying, "I don't ask where anyone comes from or what they do for a living."

"Maybe they told you their names," Fargo said. "Willard, Milton, Alonzo, Elias, and Rafer."

"I never ask for names, either."

"What do you ask for?"

Marian sat back and stared at him in mild annoyance. "The pittance I charge for them to sleep here. Their private lives are none of my business. And frankly, it's best if I don't be too friendly. Some men take that the wrong way and the next thing I know, I have to beat the simpletons off with a club."

Fargo grinned. "I bet you have to beat a lot of simpletons off."

Some of her annoyance melted. "If you only knew. I have been fighting men off since I was fourteen." Marian sighed. "I've reached the point where I am sick of it and sick of them."

"I hope not all men," Fargo said.

"There. You see? You're no different than all the rest," Marian said wearily, and once again bent to write. "Now why don't you toddle off and leave me to my work."

"I don't toddle," Fargo said, "whatever the hell that means. And I'd be obliged if you would keep an eye out for the four men and let me know if they show up."

"I thought you said there were five."

"I killed one."

Marian glanced up. "You did what?"

"I shot one of the sons of bitches over to the Lucky Lady. His name was Rafer."

She set down her pencil. "That was you? Someone came in a while ago saying there had been a shooting." Her blue

59

eyes raked him from hat to boots. "You don't look like a killer."

"You can tell just by looking at a man?" Fargo said, half-sarcastically.

"Those that hire their guns out," Marian said. "Most have a cold, hard air about them. Oh, they'll smile and act friendly but you can see it in their eyes, in how they hold themselves, in how their hands are always near their six-shooters. They are like cats about to pounce on a canary, and everyone else is the canary."

Fargo thought of Clyburn and Jareck and others of their ilk he had known. "You put that well."

"So if you're not a killer, why did you kill him?"

"Let me take you out to supper and I'll tell you all about it."

Marian snorted. "No."

"You didn't think about that, either."

"I am choosy about who I go out with."

"I'll wash and shave," Fargo said.

She grinned and shook her head. "I like cleanliness but the answer is still no."

"I'll bring flowers."

Marian's eyes twinkled with amusement. "You would buy roses for me?"

"Who said anything about buy?" Fargo said. "I'll steal them from the first garden I see."

Laughing, Marian said, "An honest man. Now that's a rarity."

"And I promise to behave," Fargo said. "Unless we run into those farmers or Robert Shanks."

The mirth left her face and her features clouded. "Why Shanks?"

"He runs things hereabouts, I hear," Fargo said. "And thinks he can ride roughshod over a friend of mine."

"And you won't let him?"

"I sure as hell will not."

"Pick me up at eight o'clock."

"You sure changed your mind quick."

"I have my reasons. Eight o'clock."

"I'll be here," Fargo promised. He smiled and touched his

hat brim and went back out and nearly bumped into Jim McCullock.

"That was mighty slick," McCullock said, and fell into step beside him.

"What?"

"Bringing up Shanks. Word is she and him don't get along."

"I didn't know."

"I've always said you were born under a four-leaf clover," McCullock joked.

They emerged and turned up the street and hadn't gone half a block when McCullock grabbed Fargo's arm and stopped dead and blurted, "Oh, hell."

Coming toward them were nearly a dozen men. Not ordinary citizens, either. At the forefront strode a dandy in the best fashion of the day. Gaudily so, for his bowler had a bright yellow band and his jacket and pants were a bright burgundy. His shoes were polished to a sheen and he twirled a cane with a gold handle and a gold tip. His face was thin and rat-like, an impression heightened by his close-set dark eyes. A thin mustache lined his upper lip and a thin beard covered his small chin. He stopped and sneered at McCullock and leaned on his cane. "Well, well, well."

Behind the dandy were Clyburn and Jareck and others stamped from the same mold. Clyburn nodded at Fargo. Jareck glared.

"Mr. Shanks," McCullock said.

"I was meaning to send for you later but now will do," Shanks said. He gave Fargo a curious scrutiny. "Introduce your friend."

"The name is Fargo," Fargo introduced himself. "And you must be Bully Bob."

The dandy's thin lips pinched. "I can't tell you how much I despise that nickname. I'd like to find out who came up with it and have them skinned alive."

"You don't do your own skinning?" Fargo said.

Shanks smiled an oily smile and tilted his head at the gun crowd behind him. "I don't need to. I can afford to hire it out."

Jareck cleared his throat. "This is the one we were tellin' you about, Mr. Shanks."

"So I gathered," Shanks said. To Fargo he said, "You don't seem to realize who I am. In case no one has told you, I run Tarryall."

"You do?" Fargo said, and tilted his head at the gun hands. "Or they do for you?"

"I like being insulted even less than I like my nickname," Shanks said.

"One of us," Fargo said, "doesn't give a good damn what you like."

Jareck started to move past Shanks but Shanks flicked his cane out, blocking him.

"No," Shanks said.

"He shouldn't ought to talk to you like that," Jareck said.

"And I said no."

Jareck colored and quickly stepped back. "Sorry, boss. He riles me, is all."

Robert Shanks gave Fargo another scrutiny and a puzzled look came over him. "There are a lot more of them than there are of you."

"You'll be first," Fargo said.

Shanks slowly nodded. "Even if you get off the first shot, and I'm doubtful you can, what have you gotten out of it? Why prod to no purpose? Why die for no good cause?"

"You run this town," Fargo said. "I run me."

After a few moments Shanks said, "You're not one of the sheep. I'll grant you that." He switched his attention to Jim McCullock. "As for you, old man, I understand you have refused my offer a second time."

"My claim ain't for sale. Ever."

"It's unfortunate you're so unreasonable," Shanks said. "Oh well." He shrugged and twirled his cane and took a step.

"We're not done," Fargo said.

Shanks drew up short.

Instantly, Clyburn came up next to him on one side and Jareck on the other and the rest of the gunnies pressed forward in a protective crescent.

"How's that again?" Shanks asked, an edge to his tone.

"The Lucky Lady," Fargo said. "We'll settle it now."

"The Lucky Lady?" Shanks repeated quizzically. He half turned and stared up the street toward the saloon and then at

Fargo. Insight dawned, and he smiled. "I'll be damned. That was you earlier?"

"Wayne said he was going to come crying to you," Fargo said.

"He did more than that," Shanks replied. "He says you're the quickest he's seen, and that includes Mr. Clyburn, here."

Clyburn regarded Fargo with renewed interest.

"Most impressive," Shanks said.

"What do you aim to do about it?" Fargo wanted to know.

"Not a thing. You might have heard that Tarryall is short on law. Hardly a week goes by that someone isn't shot or knifed or has their skull caved in." Shanks smiled that oily smile of his. "You should keep that in mind."

12

"I really need a drink," Jim McCullock remarked as the lord of Tarryall and his gun hands swaggered off down Main Street.

"Pick your whiskey mill," Fargo said. He wouldn't mind half a bottle, himself. But only half. He had a supper date later.

The first one they came to was called the Nugget. It was barely half full at that hour and they claimed a corner table. Fargo paid for a bottle and brought it and two glasses over.

McCullock was staring glumly at the floor.

"What's eating you?" Fargo asked as he slid into a chair.

"Shanks."

"I'm not worried about him coming after me," Fargo remarked.

"Not you," McCullock said. "My claim."

"You stood up to him before I got here. He might think twice with me around to lend you a hand." Which was as close to boasting as Fargo would allow.

"I know him better than you," McCullock said. "I know what he's capable of. Once he sets his sights on a claim, he always gets his hands on it."

"Always?"

McCullock accepted a glass and eagerly swallowed. "Your being here might spur him into acting sooner. Force his hand, so to speak."

"That milk's not spilt yet," Fargo said.

"I know. But I believe in plannin' ahead. I've got some serious thinking to do. I could kill him but his hired killers would riddle me before I took two steps. And before you say anything, no, I won't have you go up against him on my account."

"Shanks and me are already at odds."

"Even so." McCullock shoved the glass across for a refill, took a quick gulp, and set the glass down and turned it back and forth, his brow creased in concentration. "Yes, sir. Some serious thinking."

"When are you heading back to your claim?" Fargo brought up. "I'd like to tag along." He didn't mention his other motive: to look around for the four farmers.

"In a couple of days," McCullock said. "I have supplies to buy. And maybe something else to do."

"Oh?"

"A brainstorm is coming to me," the former quartermaster said, and smiled.

When Fargo saw that he wasn't going to explain, he sat back and raised his glass and gazed toward the batwings just as they burst open and Milton barreled into the saloon with a rifle to his shoulder. Fargo dropped the glass and dived a split second before the rifle boomed. The heavy slug tore into the back of the chair and sent it crashing over even as Fargo came down hard on his shoulder. He rolled, drew, and fired as Milton jacked the lever to feed a cartridge into the chamber. He fired as Milton got off a shot that tore into the floor inches from his face. He fired as Milton's knees buckled and he fired as Milton pitched flat.

"God Almighty," McCullock exclaimed.

The acrid odor of gun smoke in his nose, Fargo rose and went over.

Everyone was frozen in disbelief. The bartender had been pouring a drink at the bar and the liquor was splashing over the rim.

Fargo was surprised when Milton moved and groaned. He flipped him over and the farmer's eyes fluttered open and settled on him in pure hate.

"Bastard," Milton wheezed, drops of blood flecking his lips.

"Where are the others?" Fargo asked.

"They'll get you, just you wait," Milton said, and coughed.

"Not if I get to them first."

Milton was fading. He looked at the ceiling and his throat bobbed. "I came in with Rafer." He coughed some more. "I was off buyin' tobacco when you gunned him. Been followin' you ever since, waitin' my chance . . ." He stopped and gurgled and convulsed, once, and was still.

Fargo felt for a pulse. There wasn't one. He stepped back and began to reload.

The bartender came over, looking as if he would rather not. "Damnation, mister. What was that about? He came in here blazing away."

"He wanted me dead for shooting one of his friends a while ago."

Apparently everyone in town had heard about it because the bartender looked at him and said, "That was you over to the Lucky Lady?" He stared at Milton. "Two in one day. Lord Almighty."

"You fixing to tell Shanks?"

"How does this concern him?"

"It doesn't."

"Then why would I?" The bartender nodded at Milton. "I'll get in touch with the undertaker. Whatever he finds on the body will pay for the burial."

Fargo suspected the bartender would help himself to part of whatever was in Milton's pockets. As for the undertaker, he'd dump the corpse in a hole on Boot Hill. Not that he cared. His main concern now was to keep a sharp watch for the other three. It bothered him that Milton had followed him around most of the afternoon and he hadn't noticed. Granted, the streets were jammed, but that was no excuse for being careless. Returning to the table, he refilled his glass to the brim.

McCullock hadn't moved. Now he calmly raised his own glass and said, "That was close. Another of those farmers, I take it?"

Fargo nodded.

"They sure don't like you."

"The ones who are left will like me even less," Fargo said.

"Between Shanks and those corn growers, it's plumb dangerous to be around you," McCullock observed, and grinned.

Fargo would be the first to admit he had a knack for get-

66

ting into situations that put his life at risk, but he didn't find it amusing.

McCullock set down his glass and stood. "I have something I need to do. I'll meet you back at my place in an hour or so." So saying, he hurried out.

Fargo sat back and finished his whiskey. No one bothered him. The undertaker came and went, four men bearing the body out with him.

The sun was low on the horizon when Fargo stepped out into the dusty air. He headed for his friend's shack, making it a point to check behind him, often. He would be damned if he would let himself be caught unawares twice.

McCullock was already there, in the chair out front.

He smiled in greeting. "Welcome back. I've got my affairs in order so no matter what happens now, I can rest in peace."

Fargo sat on the edge of the plywood porch. He wasn't so sure he liked the sound of that and asked, "Are you planning on dying?"

"Hell no. I hope to stick around a good long while. But a fella never knows." McCullock consulted a pocket watch. "Another hour or so and you have your date with Marian. Any sprucing up you have to do, you better get to it. There's a basin inside and a pitcher of fresh water I drew just for you."

"Playing cupid, are you?" Fargo joked.

"You could do worse. I like Marian. She's a good gal."

"And you know better."

"True," McCullock said. "You're not ready to tie the knot and settle down. Hell, I doubt if you'll ever be."

"I won't make any promises to her I can't keep."

"Never said you would. But there's something you should know. It could explain why she changed her mind so sudden-like about going out with you."

Fargo waited.

"Did you notice she did it when you mentioned Shanks? I was outside her office and heard."

"I did," Fargo said.

"Well, word is she went out with him more than a few times when he first came to town. Word is, she broke it off and he wasn't happy about it."

"I don't care why she agreed to go out with me."

"You should care," McCullock said, "if it means you'll have Shanks mad at you."

"You waited until now to tell me all this?"

"I reckoned you might want to know before you go pick her up."

"Any other secrets I should know about?"

"Just this. You know about all the killings. But from time to time people also up and disappear. No one knows where they get to but one day they're here and the next they're not."

"Maybe they leave town."

"No. You don't understand. It's those who rile Bully Bob. Instead of having them shot dead and give folks more to hate him for, he arranges for them to disappear. So if I up and vanish, you'll know who to blame."

"You keep talking like something is going to happen to you."

McCullock shrugged. "We never know."

Fargo was tired of hearing about Shanks. He went inside and filled the basin. Stripping to the waist, he washed and slicked his hair. He also trimmed his beard.

In his saddlebags was a clean buckskin shirt, which he donned, and then he retied his bandanna. He slapped his hat against his leg to shake off the dust and strode back out.

Jim McCullock hadn't left his chair. "Look at you. Did you clip your nails, too?"

Fargo checked the sun. "I'd better be going."

"Watch your back."

"That goes without saying." Fargo was almost to the street when McCullock called out again.

"You did hear me say she's a good gal?"

"I don't rape women, if that's what you're worried about," Fargo grumbled. He gave a little wave and moseyed along to the Stopover.

By that time of the day most of the cots had been paid for but only about half were occupied. Marian was in her office, the ledger in front of her. She looked up when Fargo rapped on the jamb.

"You're a little early."

"I'm starving," Fargo said.

"And here I imagined it might be you were eager to see me."

"That too."

Marian closed the ledger and stood. Coming around the desk to the doorway, she took one look and teased, "You didn't have to clean up on my account."

"I washed in case you get a hankering to run your hands over my body."

She stared at him and then said flatly, "I can assure you that will never happen."

"Never is a long time," Fargo said.

13

Fargo read the menu and about choked. The prices were outrageous. But it was partly his fault they were eating at the restaurant in the Dunbar Hotel.

He had told Marian to pick any place she wanted and she'd remarked that she liked to eat at the Dunbar but could rarely afford to. Little realizing how high they jacked their prices, he'd sought to impress her by saying, "The Dunbar it will be."

Now, staring at the menu, Fargo inwardly cursed his hankering to have her. Adopting a poker face, he laid the menu flat. "Whoever owns this place must be rich as hell."

Her nose buried in her menu, Marian said much too casually, "Didn't anyone tell you? Robert Shanks is the owner."

Fargo took a sip of water and frowned. "Strange you'd want to come here. I've heard you're not too fond of him."

Marian looked up sharply. "Who told you that?"

If she could play games, Fargo reflected, he could too. "It's all over town."

"I should have expected as much, knowing how much people love to talk." Marian paused and bit her lip. "What did you hear, exactly?"

Fargo decided to have some fun. "That you and him were deeply in love and you were fixing to marry him—"

"Son of a bitch," Marian blurted, and blushed. "Sorry. That wasn't very ladylike."

"It's all right," Fargo said, smiling. "I like ladies who don't put on airs and pretend they never let a cussword cross their lips."

"Whoever told you that has it completely wrong. We weren't in love at all. At least, I certainly wasn't in love with him. As for marrying him—" Marian stopped and rolled her eyes.

"Yet here we are," Fargo said innocently, "eating at his restaurant."

"That man owns most of Tarryall," Marian replied. "There's hardly anyplace we could eat where he isn't the owner or part owner."

"We could go off into the mountains and I'll shoot a deer and butcher it," Fargo said. "Shouldn't take more than an hour or so."

"I don't want you to go to that much trouble."

"Considerate of you," Fargo said.

Marian coughed. "This will do. To be honest, I'm hoping he'll see us together."

"Is that so?" Fargo sat back. There was more going on here than she was letting on. "Are you trying to make him jealous?"

"Hell, no," Marian said. "I couldn't care less how he feels about me. But it would please me greatly for him to see I've gotten over him and I'm not afraid to go out with another man."

"Why would you be afraid?"

"Not for me. For the man I am with. Robert threatened to kill anyone I—" Marian caught herself.

"Hell," Fargo said.

"But I don't think you have anything to worry about," Marian said quickly. "Not after shooting those two men. Robert will think twice before he'll give you any trouble."

"Hell," Fargo said a second time.

"It's all over town, how you shot them. I couldn't help but hear about it."

"You're using me."

Marian's cheeks flushed red. "I am not."

"Do I look like an infant to you?"

Fidgeting in her chair, Marian said, "Well, maybe I'm using you a little. But after what he did you can't blame me."

"Which was?"

"It's personal."

"Lady, you just put me in his gun sights," Fargo said. He neglected to add that he already was. "The least you can do is explain why."

Just then the waiter came up and gave a polite bow. He was dressed in a uniform with brass buttons and a purple sash. "Would you like to place your order?"

"A bottle of whiskey and make it quick," Fargo said.

"Sir, this is a restaurant, not a saloon. We don't serve drinks by the bottle."

Fargo turned and their eyes locked. "You do now."

The waiter's throat moved up and down and he nervously fingered one of his brass buttons. "I suppose if you insist."

"I do."

The waiter anxiously shifted his weight from one foot to the other. "I could ask the manager."

Fargo slowly reached down and drew his Colt and just as slowly set it on the table with a *thunk*. "You do that."

The waiter became several shades paler than he had been. "One bottle, sir, coming right up." He bowed and imitated a jackrabbit.

Fargo slid the Colt into his holster.

"That was terrible," Marian said, but she was grinning, "scaring that poor boy like that."

"You were about to explain," Fargo reminded her.

"Oh. Yes." Marian fiddled with her menu. "I met him not long after he came to town," she said quietly. "He was polite and gentlemanly, and he dresses so fabulously."

"Fabulously," Fargo said.

"Cut it out. Anyway, he asked me out and I figured, why not? One date led to another and after a while we were seeing each other nearly every night."

"Lucky him."

"It's not what you think. We didn't do *that*."

Fargo smiled.

"You can be infuriating," Marian said. "Or is it that you like to make people squirm?"

"I'd like to make you squirm," Fargo said, and his smile widened.

"Do you want to hear about Robert and me or not?"

"I'm all ears."

Marian's jaw muscles twitched and she sniffed and said, "It got so, he considered me his. This was about the time he started to show his true colors. He'd brought in Clyburn and

Jareck and some of the others and he was going around making people pay him protection and taking over claims. And that didn't sit well with me."

Fargo guessed what was coming. "You tried to break it off and he didn't want to."

"One night we were in his suite." Marian clasped her hands in front of her. "I don't believe I've mentioned that he lives on the top floor of this very hotel, have I?"

"A lot sure skips your mind," Fargo said.

"Be nice. Anyway, he came right out and told me he'd like for me to be his wife. He didn't ask for my hand. He didn't get down on bended knee. He told me we were going to be married and that was that."

"A man who takes what he wants and everyone else be damned."

"I finally realized that, yes. I told him I wasn't about to marry him, then or ever. He told me what a big man he was going to be. How wealthy he would become. How I could have anything I wanted. All he had to do was snap his fingers and it was mine."

"You passed all that up?"

"Be nice, I said." Marian bowed her head and sighed. "How could I have been so foolish? Why didn't I see him for what he was from the outset?"

"Some people hide who they are."

"He did, and he hid it well. But that night I saw him for what he is. When I said my no was final, he grabbed me and put his hands around my throat. He actually started to squeeze and for a few seconds I thought he was going to choke me. But a strange look came over him and he let go and apologized. You'll never guess what he said next."

"That sooner or later you'd change your mind."

"How did you know?" Marian said, nodding. "He said that he could afford to be patient, and since then he comes around every few days just to talk, as he puts it, and to ask if I'm ready to say I do."

"He won't give up so long as you stay here."

"I fear you're right. He's had his men spying on me. I've seen them. When I've confronted him and demanded to know why, he smiles and tells me it's all in my head."

Marian clenched her fists. "It's so frustrating. And so very infuriating."

"How does he feel about you going out with other men?"

"I'm getting to that." Marian cleared her throat. "He doesn't like it. He doesn't like it at all. Several men have asked me out but I only went out with each of them once. Two disappeared and the third man showed up at the Stopover all black and blue and said he wasn't interested in me anymore."

"Yet here we sit."

Marian nodded. "It came to me that if anyone could stand up to him, it would be you."

"Thanks," Fargo said. He wasn't as annoyed as he sounded. Trouble was brewing with Shanks over Jim McCullock's claim, anyway. But he didn't like being made her pawn. "You could have told me all this when I asked you out."

"I know. You must hate me."

"I'd have to be loco to hate a woman with a body like yours."

Marian's color deepened. "You come right out with it, don't you?"

"A man doesn't get up a woman's skirts by beating around her belt."

"You have no shame," Marian said. "I don't know whether to be flattered or insulted."

"It's not an insult for a man to want you."

"That depends on the man, and on *how* he wants a woman. In that regard you're as straightforward as Shanks."

"Except I give the lady a choice," Fargo said, "and I haven't strangled one in a coon's age."

Marian grinned. "I didn't say him and you are alike. Quite the contrary."

"Well, now that we have that out of the way—"

Just then the waiter bustled up bearing a bottle and two glasses. He set them down with a flourish and declared, "Compliments of the house, sir."

Fargo picked up the bottle. It was the best Monongahela money could buy. "I get this free?"

"With the owner's compliments, sir," the waiter said, and gestured.

At the rear of the dining room were double doors into the

kitchen, and in front of them stood Robert Shanks, resplendent in a fine suit and polished boots. Shanks smiled and gave a bow of his own.

"Oh God," Marian said.

"Mr. Shanks said for you to enjoy yourselves," the waiter related. "He said that the bottle and your meal are on him."

"Thank him," Fargo said, "and tell him I pay for my own meals."

The waiter was astounded. "You're refusing his kind offer?"

"We are," Marian said.

"And tell him that if I catch one of his gun hands following us," Fargo said, "I'll make it three in one day."

"I don't understand," the waiter said.

"Your boss will." Fargo flicked his fingers. "Scoot."

The waiter hurried to the rear. Shanks never lost his smile but they saw his face harden. Wheeling, Shanks went into the kitchen.

"Why did you provoke him like that?" Marian asked. "He'll be out for your blood."

"He's welcome to try," Fargo said.

14

The rest of their meal passed pleasantly.

Fargo had an inch-thick slab of juicy elk meat with potatoes covered in gravy, along with peas and carrots and bread fresh from the oven. For dessert he chose a slice of cherry pie. He ate so much, he downed only half the bottle of Monongahela.

"You sure have an appetite," Marian complimented him as he was finishing the pie.

"For more than food," Fargo said with a wink.

"You never stop thinking about that, do you?"

"Only when I'm awake."

Marian laughed. "And when you're asleep you dream about it."

"Not so much." Fargo didn't have many dreams. That he remembered, anyway.

"I want to thank you," Marian said, sipping a glass of rum. "I've had a marvelous time."

"The night is young."

Marian took a healthier swallow. "Let's not get ahead of ourselves. I'm not the kind of woman you apparently think I am."

"The kind who likes to make love?"

"You, sir, are incorrigible," Marian said, but not unkindly.

They hadn't seen any more sign of Robert Shanks. Nor did Fargo spot Shanks's hired guns trailing after them as they made their way up the street.

The night air was chill and Marian pulled her shawl around her shoulders. "I'm sorry I brought you into this, Skye."

"I'm not."

"You almost sound as if you want Shanks to try something."

Fargo did. He'd like an excuse. Any excuse. It beat waiting around for the other shoe to drop.

"My house is behind the Stopover," Marian mentioned. "It makes it easy on me, coming and going to work."

The night was serene. Stars shimmered in the firmament. Piano music and muted voices carried on the breeze. So did the smell of cigar smoke from an open window.

"It's almost peaceful, isn't it?" Marian remarked.

As if to prove her wrong a shot blasted in one of the saloons and a woman screamed.

"I did say almost," Marian said.

"Why not sell out and move back East? You'd be safe from Shanks."

"I like it here," Marian said, and breathed deep of the night air. "I like the atmosphere, if that makes sense. It's wild. It's exciting." As if she had revealed too much she quickly added, "I like the mountains, too. The forests and the lakes. And the wildlife. The bears and the chipmunks."

Fargo snorted.

"What, I can't like chipmunks?"

"I know I do."

Marian grinned. "You have a knack for putting a woman at ease."

"The easier to get their clothes off," Fargo said.

"About that," Marian said hesitantly, and took a few more strides. "It's too soon. I would like to, I'm ashamed to admit. But I can't."

"Some things can't be rushed."

"You're awful understanding."

No, Fargo was awful horny, but he was also patient. "Take your time making up your mind."

As they neared the Stopover she said, "I need to check on things."

Almost all the cots were filled and the long room rumbled to snores.

Marian led Fargo down an aisle. A lamp was kept lit at the back for those who needed to use the outhouse. Beyond, they came to a fence with a gate, and past that stood a modest two-story house. On the porch she fiddled with her shawl and seemed reluctant to part company.

"Thank you for a fine evening."

"Any time," Fargo said, and pecked her on the cheek. He figured that was the end of it for the night but she seized him by the shoulders and pressed her mouth to his in a fierce kiss. Suddenly stepping back, she turned and hurried inside as if afraid he would pursue her.

Fargo grinned and went down the steps. He crossed to the gate and along the path to the Stopover. Rather than go through it he went around and as he came to the front a silhouette separated from a darker patch of shadow. Instantly, his hand was on his Colt.

"No need for that," Clyburn said, coming into the light cast from the window with his hands out from his sides.

Fargo probed the surrounding darkness.

"I'm alone," Clyburn said.

"I warned Shanks not to have us followed."

"Do you think I'd stoop to that?" Clyburn said. "He sent me with an invite."

"I'm listening."

"He'd like you to pay him a visit at the Dunbar. He's on the top floor."

"Why should I?" Fargo said.

Clyburn shrugged. "Makes no difference to me what you do. He wanted me to say that he has a proposition for you that's worth your while. His own words."

"What kind of proposition?"

Again the man in the black hat and jacket shrugged. "He didn't tell me and I didn't ask."

Fargo debated whether to go. He didn't trust Robert Shanks any farther than he could throw the hotel, but it might be worth the bother to find out what he wanted.

He motioned. "Walk ahead of me."

"I'm no back-shooter," Clyburn said indignantly, but he ambled off, his spurs jingling.

Fargo stayed a few feet behind, his hand never leaving the Colt.

"I heard about the second gent you shot today," Clyburn remarked.

Fargo didn't say anything.

"You've sure impressed Mr. Shanks," Clyburn went on. "He's never treated anyone with the respect he's treating you."

"From what I hear," Fargo said, "he doesn't treat anyone with respect."

"You've been listening to his filly," Clyburn said. "He's a powerful man in these parts and tends to do as he pleases. That upsets her."

"So do the killings and the people who disappear."

Clyburn looked over his shoulder, and grinned. "I wouldn't know about that."

The Dunbar's lobby was quiet after the hubbub of the street. Wide stairs led to a landing and from there they climbed to the top floor.

A gun hand was leaning against a wall, his thumbs hooked in his gun belt. He nodded at Clyburn.

"There's always a guard," Clyburn said to Fargo. "No one is allowed up without Mr. Shanks's say-so."

The hall floor was covered with carpet, not hardwood like the floors below. Clyburn walked to a white door and opened it and stepped aside. "After you."

"Hired killers first," Fargo said.

"I told you I don't back-shoot," Clyburn muttered, but he went in.

To the right was a fireplace topped by a wide mantel. The furniture was the kind that would cost a year's wages for most people. Near the fireplace was a small table, and Jareck and two others were playing cards. All of them stood.

"You're back," Jareck stated the obvious.

"Let him know," Clyburn said.

"He already does," Jareck said, and nodded at a door across the room.

Through it came Tarryall's self-styled lord and master in a blue dinner jacket and a white shirt. "I heard you come in," Robert Shanks said. Smiling, he held out his hand and waited for Fargo to take it.

Fargo just stood there.

"You have nothing to worry about," Shanks said. "I invited you here under a flag of truce, you might say."

Fargo still didn't shake.

"Have it your way," Shanks said, and sighed and lowered his arm. "But must you always be such a hard-ass?"

"You threatened my friend," Fargo said.

"Which is precisely what I want to discuss." Shanks went behind a bar and produced a bottle and two glasses. "I understand you're fond of Monongahela."

"Been checking up on me?"

"There's a saying I'm fond of," Shanks said as he poured. "Know your friends well but know your enemies better."

Fargo motioned at the shooters. "What was that about not having anything to worry about?"

"Not at this moment, no. And perhaps not later on, either, if we can come to an arrangement." Shanks brought the glasses over and held one out.

Fargo accepted it.

"Mr. Clyburn," Shanks said. "I want you and Mr. Jareck and the others to go into the next room and stay there until I call for you."

"Is that wise, boss?" Jareck said.

"Are you calling me stupid?"

"No. Never. I just mean this hombre could be dangerous."

"There is no *could be*," Shanks said. "But you needn't worry. He won't shoot me."

"How do you know?" Jareck said.

"Because I'm unarmed and he's not the kind to shoot a defenseless man in cold blood." Shanks smiled at Fargo. "Are you?"

Fargo had to hand it to him. Shanks could read people like they were books.

"I'll take that as a yes," Shanks said, and snapped his fingers at the gun crowd. "Why are you still here?"

Clyburn went last and closed the door behind them.

"Now then," Shanks said, moving to a settee. "Why don't we have a seat and discuss our differences like civilized men?"

Fargo roosted at the opposite end. Shifting so he could keep an eye on both doors, he sipped and said, "Let's get this over with."

"Always to the point. I like that." Shanks placed his left

foot on his right knee and draped his left arm across the back of the settee. "I have a proposition for you. It involves your friend, Mr. McCullock, and Miss Marian Hatcher."

Fargo realized that was the first he'd heard Marian's last name.

"I don't know if she's told you but she and I came close to being engaged."

"I hear she said no."

"Women," Shanks said. "You know how fickle they can be. She doesn't know her own mind but she will given time. And if she doesn't see other men."

"That should be up to her and the other men."

"Yes, well," Shanks said. "The way I see it, I have a perfect right to protect my interests. And to that end, I'm willing to make you an offer I've never made before." He paused. "You're aware of another interest of mine, namely, your friend's claim. I'd like to buy it and he doesn't want to sell."

"What does she have to do with him?"

"Simply this." Shanks smiled. "I'm willing to drop my interest in him if you're willing to drop your interest in her. What do you say?"

15

Fargo barely held his temper in check. He had to hand it to Shanks; being unarmed was the smartest thing the man could have done.

"What do you say?" Bully Bob again prompted when he didn't get an answer.

"I have a better notion. Leave him alone and leave her alone."

Shanks frowned and sat back. "I was hoping you'd be reasonable."

"I am."

Shanks took a swallow of whiskey, his eyes glinting with resentment. "I offer to do you a favor and you refuse to do me one."

"I don't barter with people's lives."

"Aren't you the noble bastard?" Shanks snapped. "But if you think I'm going to let you throw dirt in my face, you have another think coming."

Fargo set his glass on a table and stood. "Thanks for the drink." He started toward the door but Shanks wasn't done.

"I did some checking on you. They say you have grit. They say you're good with that Colt of yours. So out of respect I met with you man to man, and you do this."

"Let it go."

"I can't," Shanks said. "I want her more than I've ever wanted anything. I could have any female in Tarryall but she's the one I want most. I can't explain it. It's just how it is."

"She doesn't want you."

"She told you that?" Shanks gestured as if it were of no consequence. "She doesn't have to want me. She'll get used to me, in time, and that's all that counts." He emptied his glass and smacked it on the table. "As for your friend, Mr. McCullock, I'll get around to him eventually."

"Eventually?" Fargo said.

"I'm no fool. You can't hang around here forever. In time you'll drift elsewhere and that's when I'll make my move."

Fargo faced him. "You harm Mac and I'll come back."

"You do and I'll be ready for you," Shanks said. "And the next time I won't be nice like I'm being now."

Fargo went to the door.

"The same holds true for her," Shanks said. "You'll drift on and she'll still be here and I'll still be here." He uttered a bark of cold mirth. "All you've done is delay things."

Fargo jerked the door open and slammed it after him. The hell of it was, Shanks was right. He had no intention of staying in Tarryall the rest of his days.

At the lobby he stopped to collect himself. He mustn't forget the farmers. Willard, Alonzo, and Elias were still out there, somewhere, and might take it into their heads to try to do what Milton and Rafer couldn't.

Squaring his shoulders, Fargo drifted out into the night. He made it a point to stay close to the buildings as he went down the street.

Tarryall's wild life was in full swing. Every saloon was jammed. Liquor was being guzzled by the gallon and every vice imaginable was being plied. Laughter, voices, the tinkle of poker chips were constant.

The crack of a rifle was louder.

Lead smacked the wall near Fargo's face and slivers stung his cheek. Dropping into a crouch, he palmed the Colt. The shot had come from across the street.

Passersby were stopping and looking around in confusion.

Again the rifle boomed. This time the slug dug into the boardwalk next to Fargo's boot. He caught the muzzle flash on the roof of a building across from him. Fanning two quick shots, he darted into the street, zigzagging to make it harder for the assassin to hit him. Men and women gave way and a rider reined his horse aside. A third blast, and cries broke out and people ran every which way.

Fargo was almost to an overhang. He snapped off a shot at a hunched silhouette. In reply the rifle crashed, and lead missed him by a few inches.

Darting around the corner, Fargo headed for the rear. He figured the man on the roof would come down that way, and he would be waiting. At the back he halted and peered around. There were no stairs and he didn't see a ladder. He wondered if the rifleman had gotten up there from inside. But the building was a mercantile and it was closed and dark.

Fargo sidled along the wall and came to a door and found his answer. It had been busted open with a pry bar or some other tool. He pushed, and it swung in with a loud squeak.

Inside, the rifle thundered. Splinters flew, and Fargo flattened. He crawled inside behind a shelf of dry goods and warily rose.

Out front there were shouts and a commotion.

Fargo scanned the ceiling for some sign of his would-be killer. He spied a flight of narrow stairs and crept toward them. Suddenly, at the front of the store, the rifle spat more lead. Fargo heard the buzz of a miss, and responded with a swift shot.

Boots drummed. There was the tinkle of a tiny bell and the front door opened. For a split second a large bulk filled the doorway.

Fargo raised his Colt but the bulk was gone. He gave chase and had the presence of mind not to mindlessly run out. Instead, he slowed and poked his head past the jamb.

The street was deserted except for a man in a buckboard and another in a bowler who appeared paralyzed with fear.

Fargo looked right and left and didn't see anyone running off. He slipped out, his back to the window, unsure of which way to go.

The man in the bowler pointed at the corner Fargo had gone around not two minutes ago. "He went down there," he said.

Fargo ran over. At the far end someone was going around the building. "Damn it," he spat, and ran after them. Once again he was careful not to blunder into a hailstorm of lead, and looked first.

The assassin was gone.

Fargo swore, and reloaded. He suspected it had been one of the farmers. Willard, maybe, judging by the man's size. But then again, Robert Shanks had several good-sized gun hands on his payroll. Shanks's talk about waiting him out may have been a ruse so he wouldn't expect trouble.

He wouldn't put anything past that son of a bitch.

The street was filling when Fargo came out. The man with the bowler was still there, pasty faced, and smiled thinly.

"Did you get a good look at him?" Fargo asked.

"No. Sorry," the townsman said. "Just a glimpse. All I can tell you is that he was big and he moved awful fast."

"Did you see what he was wearing?"

"His clothes? No. He was a blur. I could see he had a rifle but that was all."

"I'm obliged."

"One thing," the townsman said.

Fargo stopped.

"I could be mistaken, you understand. But his hat was sort of funny-looking."

"Funny how?"

"I only had that glimpse, mind you," the man said. "But I'd swear it was almost too small for a man that big." He smiled timidly. "If that helps any."

Fargo thanked him and strode off. Large man, small hat—it sounded like Willard. The other two, Alonzo and Elias, could have been anywhere, waiting their chance.

Light glowed in the window of the former quartermaster's shack. One eye on the street, Fargo pounded on the door.

McCullock opened it, and smiled. "No need for you to knock. Walk right in, anytime."

Fargo claimed a chair. It had been a long day and fatigue gnawed at his body. He pushed his hat back and rubbed his eyes and when he opened them, McCullock had a bottle for him.

"Bought this just for you."

"Tarryall is Monongahela heaven," Fargo remarked. Opening it, he tilted it to his mouth.

Humming to himself, McCullock sat and held out his hand. "I wouldn't mind a sip myself."

"You're in a good mood," Fargo observed.

"Why shouldn't I be?" McCullock drank and wiped his mouth. "So tell me. How did your supper with the lovely Miss Hatcher go?"

"It's not her you need to hear about," Fargo said, and related his invite to the Dunbar and the gist of his words with Robert Shanks.

"So he aims to wait you out, does he?" McCullock said. "Clever of the bastard."

"He's not stupid," Fargo conceded.

McCullock thoughtfully rubbed his stubble. "How long do you reckon you can stick around?"

Fargo was honest with him. "A week at the most." He had an appointment to keep in Santa Fe at the end of the month.

"That gives us a little time, anyhow."

"For what?"

"To do some panning and digging for gold." McCullock grinned. "Yes, sir. This promises to be right interesting."

"You're taking this a lot better than I thought you would."

"You having to leave? Hell. I knew you couldn't stay forever. It's enough that you showed up when you did. Like I told you, you're an answer to my prayers."

"Some answer," Fargo said.

McCullock went over to a shelf and brought back a deck of cards that had seen a lot of use. "How about a few friendly hands before we turn in?"

"Why not?"

Humming, McCullock shuffled and began to deal.

Fargo hated to quash his friend's mood but he brought up, "It's him or you. You know that, don't you?"

"What do you want me to do? Cry? Pull out what little hair I've got left?" McCullock chuckled. "No, it's him or me, root hog or die. All I have to do is make sure it's not me."

"Did that brainstorm you mentioned give you an idea how to do that?"

"Prayer," Jim McCullock said, and laughed.

16

The next day at noon they headed for Crooked Creek.

McCullock led a pack mule laden with tools and supplies. He was in fine spirits, and as they left Tarryall behind and started up a dirt road fringed by thick timber, he took to humming again. "Rock of Ages," of all things.

Fargo followed. Time and again he shifted in the saddle to check their back trail. He was glad to be in the wilds again. He'd always felt more at home in the mountains and on the plains than in a town or city. Part of it was the solitude. He didn't need to be around other people all the time, like some did. The other part was his wanderlust. He always yearned to see what lay over the next hill, the next mountain, the next horizon.

They traveled northwest until they were in the mountains and followed Tarryall Creek to where it branched. All along Tarryall they passed claim after claim. Men in water up to their knees were panning for color. Others worked sluice boxes or dug with pick and shovel. Unfriendly stares were thrown at anyone who came too close. Some claims were protected by guards with rifles.

Fargo reckoned that by the time they reached Crooked Creek the claims would dwindle. It was the opposite. Every square foot was spoken for. To say there was barely elbow space wasn't an understatement.

Overtaking his friend, Fargo ventured to bring up, "How can you be sure no one has settled on your claim while you were gone?"

"I filed on it, legal and proper. Anyone tries to steal it is fair game."

"Do many forget to file?"

"Less than you'd imagine. Most at least have the sense to register. Those as don't only have themselves to blame if their claim is stolen out from under them."

"Let me guess who does most of the stealing," Fargo said.

"Shanks is a genius at it. I'll give him that," McCullock said. "Most times, he buys the owners off like he tried to buy me."

"He wouldn't ever buy me off," Fargo declared.

"Like I've said," McCullock responded, "an answer to my prayers."

It was eight miles to the claim. The sun was low on the western horizon when they rounded a bend and McCullock drew rein. "There she is," he proudly announced, and pointed.

It wasn't the biggest. It wasn't the smallest. Stakes had been pounded into the ground and notices attached informing one and all who the claim belonged to. There was a sluice box that didn't appear to have seen a lot of use and a lean-to for shelter from the elements.

"She's not much but we'll make do," McCullock said.

"Why do you keep calling it 'she'?"

"I named her Mabel after the sweetest gal I ever met, back when I was young and spry like you."

"How come you never asked for her hand?"

"I did. Several times. She always turned me down. Said as how I wasn't stable enough. And me with a regular job with the army."

"Could be she was thinking of your hair and your hide."

"It was my hair and my hide, not hers. I liked what I did. So when she begged me to quit, I said no."

"Yet you name a claim after her."

"She was special, Skye. I'd look at her and swear I tasted honey in my mouth."

"You had it bad, you old coon."

"I don't deny it," McCullock said. "She was the best thing that ever happened to me but it wasn't meant to be."

They reined up at the lean-to.

Fargo slid off and stretched and walked to the creek. The water was muddied from all the panning and sluicing going on. "Do you really think there's gold here?"

"I know there is or I wouldn't have filed. First week I was here I filled half a poke. Found a few nuggets in with the color."

"How big?"

"Not much more than pea size," McCullock admitted. "But gold is gold."

"And piss is piss."

"Are you saying I'm wrong to expect to find more?"

"Hell, I hope you get rich, you old coon," Fargo said.

Squatting, he dipped his hands in the water and splashed some on his face. It was cold and invigorating.

"We'll strip our animals and I'll get supper cooking," McCullock proposed.

"You don't want to pan a spell or work your sluice?"

"Plenty of time for that tomorrow."

Fargo was mildly surprised. Most of those afflicted with the gold hunger were fanatics. They'd work from dawn until it was too dark to see and be reluctant to stop.

Over stew and biscuits McCullock remarked that the next claim downstream from his belonged to two men from Ohio. "Friendly gents, so don't go shooting them."

Fargo had noticed the pair earlier. "What about upstream?"

"A green kid from Mississippi or some such," McCullock revealed. "He's not friendly. Seems to think everyone is out to fleece him."

Fargo gazed up the creek. "No sign of him now."

"That's sort of peculiar," McCullock said. "He never leaves, that I know of. But maybe he had to go out for vittles and whatnot."

Stars blossomed, and they were a wonder to behold. That high up, the sky was clear as the finest crystal.

In Denver or even Tarryall there might appear to be hundreds, here there were thousands, a celestial spectacle that Fargo never tired of admiring.

They turned in early.

Fargo spread his blankets and leaned back on his saddle and thought about Marian Hatcher. She was safe until he left, but what then? Would Shanks force her to marry him against her will? He wouldn't put anything past that son of a bitch.

Across the fire under his own blankets, McCullock did more infernal humming.

"You keep that up and you'll wear your throat out," Fargo grumbled.

McCullock chuckled. "They say that folks who are touchy about sounds are prickly by nature."

"I'm as good-natured as the next gent," Fargo said.

"I've known you a good many years and good-natured isn't how I'd describe you."

"How would you?"

McCullock looked across the flames at him. "You're the toughest bastard I know, and that's no lie."

"I've known tougher."

"Apaches, maybe. But there isn't a white man breathing who can claim to have as much bark on them as you do."

"You want me to loan you money? Is that why all this flattery?"

McCullock laughed. "You've done me the biggest favor ever by showing up when you did. I wouldn't take a cent from you."

"Fat lot of good I've done so far."

"There's always tomorrow," McCullock said, and rolled over.

"Did you bring any whiskey?"

"No. You'll have to stay sober for a few days."

"Some friend you are." Fargo placed his hands on his chest and closed his eyes. The rarified air, the good food, the friendly banter, had him relaxed and drowsy. In no time he drifted off and slept his first deep, good sleep in days.

As was his long habit, he woke at the first pink blush of predawn and lay listening to the birds greet the new day.

Down the creek a pot clinked. One of the two men from Ohio was puttering about.

Fargo's own stomach growled. Sitting up, he stretched, then cast off his blanket, got the coffeepot, and walked to the creek. It was barely five feet wide and in the dry season so shallow that a man could stick a finger in and not get the finger completely wet. He filled the pot and was turning when he caught sight of an orange glow high on the slope across the way. Someone was camped on the next mountain. It could have been a gold hunter. It could have been a hunter. Or it could have been someone else.

It was that "someone else" that bothered him.

The coffee was perking and Fargo had cracked some eggs and was sizzling bacon when Jim McCullock rolled over.

"Damn, that smells good."

"Figured you aimed to sleep the day away," Fargo said. "The sun's already up."

"This old body isn't as lively as it used to be." McCullock slowly sat up and shook himself. "And the mornin' chill is harder to take."

"You'll feel better with some food in you."

"Bring it on. I am starved enough to eat a horse, saddle and all."

They had finished breakfast and were sitting there talking when boots crunched on the gravel and the two men from Ohio approached. Fargo had seen their ilk countless times: city men, soft of sinew, wearing clothes ill suited to the mountains. They looked enough alike to be brothers. Each had a rifle.

"Floyd and Lloyd," McCullock greeted them, with a nod at each. "How have you boys been?"

"Working hard," Floyd answered.

"And keeping our rifles close," Lloyd said.

"Something happen?" McCullock asked.

Floyd nodded. "Young Spense, that boy from Mississippi. You haven't heard?"

"I saw he wasn't working his claim," McCullock mentioned.

"Some men showed up the other day," Lloyd said. "Told us not to go anywhere near it. Told us he'd been bought out."

"You'll never guess by who," Floyd said.

McCullock scowled. "Who else but Bully Bob Shanks?"

"One and the same," Lloyd confirmed.

"Next he'll try to buy out you or us," Floyd predicted.

"He's already set to work on me," McCullock informed them. "But he's not eager to tangle with my pard, here." He introduced Fargo.

"So you're Jim's new partner?" Floyd said.

"You'd best be careful, mister," Lloyd said. "That Shanks will stop at nothing to get what he wants. A lot of men have up and disappeared."

Floyd nodded. "No trace was ever found."

"We have to have eyes in the back of our head," Lloyd said bitterly.

"And even that's not enough," Floyd said. "It could happen to any of us at any time."

"If someone disappears around here," Fargo said, "it won't be me."

17

His vow proved prophetic.

The morning went by without incident. They worked the sluice and panned. It was McCullock who suddenly cried, "Eureka!" and rushed over, beaming, to show Fargo a flake about the size of a double-eagle in the bottom of his pan. "Look! I told you I picked a good spot."

Another hour of panning turned up a few specks and one small flake.

McCullock waded out, set his pan down, and announced that he would be back in a bit. "Nature calls," he said, and walked off into the pines.

Fargo went on panning. It was fifteen or twenty minutes before he looked up, wondering why McCullock was taking so long. He panned for another five minutes or so, then waded out, placed his pan next to McCullock's, and walked halfway to the timber. "Jim?" he called.

Down the creek Floyd and Lloyd stopped working and looked in his direction.

Fargo moved to the trees. Cupping his hand to his mouth, he shouted, "Jim! Where are you?"

There was no answer.

Fargo was puzzled, and a little concerned. His friend wouldn't have gone that far. He shouted McCullock's name a few more times.

Floyd and Lloyd came hurrying up, and the former asked, "What's wrong?"

"Where did he get to?" asked Lloyd. "Do you think something has happened to him?"

"How the hell would I know?" Fargo growled in annoyance, and stalked into the forest. The ground was covered with pine needles and old leaves. He found deer tracks and elk tracks and a patch of bare earth with the partial print of a bear paw, many days old. But no footprints.

"Let's spread out," Lloyd suggested.

A hundred yards farther, Fargo stopped. This was getting them nowhere. They could search for a month of Sundays and not find him. He cupped his hand and yelled at the top of his lungs, "McCullock! Answer me, damn you!"

He got a reply but not the one he wanted.

"Over here!" Floyd shouted, frantically waving. "I've found something."

Fargo reached him a few steps ahead of Lloyd and both of them stared at a torn strip of shirt in Floyd's hand.

"I found this lying here. Was this what he was wearing?"

Snatching it, Fargo felt a chill come over him. There was a fresh blood stain. "It's his, all right."

"But where's the rest of it?" Floyd wondered.

"And where is he?" Lloyd said.

"Fan out," Fargo directed. Growing more anxious by the minute, he roved in ever wider circles. All he found were a few smudges and scuff marks. He examined the piece of shirt again and discovered something he'd missed: a slit above the stain, a cut made by a knife. "Damn," he said softly.

Floyd and Lloyd came back, Floyd shaking his head. "It's like looking for a needle in a haystack."

"Only harder," Lloyd said.

Fargo refused to give up. He urged them to keep hunting.

Half an hour went by.

An hour.

Fargo called a stop and the three of them converged. The expressions on Floyd and Lloyd said all there was to say.

Fargo headed back. He suggested they saddle up and search a bigger area.

"We'd be wasting our time," Lloyd predicted.

"Poor Jim has up and vanished into thin air, just like those others," Floyd said.

Fargo showed them the slit. "Still think it was thin air?"

"Good God!" Lloyd exclaimed. "He was murdered!"

"They must have snuck up and stabbed him before he could shout for help," was Lloyd's assessment.

Fargo was simmering. Some help he'd been. He shouldn't have let McCullock stray off by his lonesome. "Would you two mind watching his claim for me?"

"Where will you be?" Floyd asked. "Searching?"

"I'm going to pay a visit to the son of a bitch who did this." Fargo was sure it was Shanks. He remembered the campfire on the mountain the night before. It must have been some of Shanks's men. That business about Shanks waiting him out had been a lie. He should have known better.

"I'll miss that old coot," Lloyd remarked. "He treated us decent."

Fargo slipped the Ovaro's bridle on.

"He sure was easy to get along with," Floyd said. "Others out here aren't nearly so friendly."

Fargo smoothed the saddle blanket and swung the saddle up and over. He was done with the cinch and about to climb on when he remembered the two pans by the creek. He retrieved them and placed them in the lean-to.

"Don't you worry," Floyd said. "We won't let anything happen to your gear."

Fargo inwardly winced. He'd said the same thing to McCullock. Stepping into the stirrups, he settled himself. "Anyone comes near this claim, shoot them."

"Sorry?" Lloyd said.

"You heard me," Fargo said, and went to rein around.

"I don't know if we can do that," Floyd said. "Shoot somebody, I mean. Neither of us has ever hurt anyone."

Lloyd nodded. "We have rifles but I doubt we could use them unless someone was trying to kill us."

"Then get word to me."

"Where will we find you?" Lloyd asked.

Fargo thought about it. "McCullock's shack." He told them how to find it. Then, with a jab of his spurs, he headed for Tarryall.

Without a packhorse to slow him, he made it in half the time. He rode straight to the Dunbar, drew up at the hitch rail, and dismounted. Out of the corner of his eye he saw a beanpole with a revolver near the entrance. The man saw him, too, and hurried inside.

Several women in bright dresses were seated in the lobby,

talking. Two men were by a pillar. The desk clerk was checking someone in and didn't notice when Fargo crossed to the stairs.

At the top was another gun hand. It wasn't the same one who had been there the night before. "Stop right there, mister," he commanded. "This floor is private."

"I'm here to see Shanks," Fargo said. "Tell him I'm here."

"Can't."

"Why the hell not?"

"Because he's not in. He's off on business, and told me not to expect him back until late."

Fargo believed him. "When he shows up tell him he has until morning to bring my friend to me."

"Your friend?"

"Jim McCullock. Shanks knows who he is. Dead or alive, I want him. And if he's dead . . ." Fargo didn't finish.

"Was that a threat?"

"It sure as hell was." Wheeling, Fargo descended. As he emerged from the lobby he realized how careless he was being. Shanks wasn't his only enemy. The three farmers were still out there somewhere.

Reins in hand, he walked the Ovaro to the Stopover. Marian wasn't in her office and a man sweeping the floor said he had no idea when she'd be back.

"Figures," Fargo muttered.

His next stop was the shack. The front door was ajar, and he remembered McCullock closing it when they left.

Palming his Colt, he pushed. No shots thundered. He poked his head in.

The place was empty, and everything seemed to be in order.

Puzzled, Fargo entered and shut the door. McCullock's bottle was in the cupboard. Forgoing a glass, he sat at the table and sucked down bug juice. He'd made good headway when there was a knock on the door. "It's not bolted," he hollered.

In came a two-legged church mouse in a stiff-collared black coat and a derby. Spectacles were perched on the tip of his nose and under his arm was a black leather valise. "Pardon me, but is Mr. McCullock home?"

"Do you see him anywhere?"

"No, I do not."

"Then he must not be here."

The man coughed. "Oh. I see. That's a shame. But this is his shack, is it not? I have the right address, don't I?"

"Do you?" Fargo retorted.

"Is it me, sir, or are you in a bad temper?"

"You have no idea," Fargo said.

"Well, I wish you wouldn't take it out on me. I'm here as a favor to Mr. McCullock."

"You came to talk him to death?"

"No. I stopped by to drop off his papers. It will save him a visit to my office."

"And who might you be?"

The man took off his derby. "Abercrombie P. Finch, at your service."

"That's some handle," Fargo said. "What does the P stand for?"

"Phineas."

"Your name fits you."

"Why, thank you. I'm an attorney by the way," Finch revealed. "Mr. McCullock came to see me yesterday about preparing certain papers, which we did. We had them notarized. I was to attend to a few minor details and he was to return to pick them up, but since I happened to be in this part of town I thought I would be a Good Samaritan."

"Do you walk on water, too?"

"Here now," Finch said, and harrumphed. "How soon do you expect him?"

"Maybe never."

"I beg your pardon?"

Fargo told him about the ride to the claim and its aftermath. "We looked and looked but couldn't find him. I aim to keep at it until I find out what happened."

"How terrible," Finch said, and came over. "Do you mind if I have a seat? It was a long walk and I'm not accustomed to much exercise."

"Could have fooled me."

"Sir?"

"Help yourself."

The lawyer pulled out the other chair. "I haven't caught your name, but are you by any chance Mr. Fargo? Mr. Skye Fargo?"

"If I am?"

"It would be marvelously fortuitous."

"Can you say that in small words?"

Finch placed the valise on the table and unfastened the straps. "He told me that something might happen to him."

"Who did?"

"Why, Mr. McCullock. Who else? He informed me of his claim on Crooked Creek and how worried he was. I'm familiar with the shootings and knifings and the disappearances so I understand why he took the precaution he did."

"You could talk rings around a tree," Fargo said irritably. He wanted to be left to his drinking.

"With remarkable foresight, as it turns out, Mr. McCullock took steps to prevent his claim from falling into the wrong hands."

"Steps?" Fargo said.

"Specifically, he made out a will."

"You don't say. Does he have kin somewhere? I think he mentioned a brother once."

"He didn't leave his claim to his brother, Mr. Fargo. Didn't he tell you?"

"Get to the goddamned point before my head explodes."

"Certainly." Finch beamed. "Mr. McCullock left it to you."

"What?"

"Congratulations. You are now the legal owner of your very own gold claim."

18

Fargo sat there staring at the lawyer for a good minute before he said, "The hell you say."

"It was Mr. McCullock's express wish," Abercrombie Phineas Finch said. "He practically burst into my office, he was so excited to draw up his will."

Fargo needed another chug of whiskey.

"All proper papers have been duly recorded," Finch assured him. "No one can file on it and take the claim away from you."

"My own gold claim," Fargo said in disbelief.

"It's remarkable that Mr. McCullock should disappear so soon after making the will out. Perhaps he had a premonition of danger."

"That premonition, as you call it, is Robert Shanks."

"Ah. Yes. Well." Finch coughed and opened the valise and took out a document. He slid it across. "Here is your copy of the will."

Fargo looked at it without really seeing the words.

"If you don't mind my saying, you seem a bit stunned. Not that I blame you. Not many people have a gold claim fall into their lap."

"I can do anything with it I want?"

"Anything at all," Finch said with a smile. "It's completely and legally yours."

Fargo tapped the papers. "Do I owe you any money for any of this?"

"No. Mr. McCullock paid for everything in advance. He had it all worked out down to the dollar."

"He would," Fargo said. As quartermaster, it had been

McCullock's job to pass out uniforms and provisions to the troops. It involved a lot of bookkeeping and tallying.

"He remarked that he was looking ahead and unfortunately it turns out he was right." Finch stood. "I've taken enough of your time, and I have other clients to see." He extended his hand. "Congratulations on your good fortune."

It was like shaking an empty sock. Fargo watched the lawyer go, then leaned back in his chair and took several long swallows.

This changed everything. He couldn't just ride off as he'd intended. Maybe, he reflected, that was Mac's idea all along.

"A goddamn gold claim," Fargo said, and gave bent to a laugh that died in his throat. On an angry impulse he got up, folded the will and stuck it under his shirt, and went out. He was unwrapping the Ovaro's reins when who should come strolling up the street but the man he was going to see and his flock of gun hawks.

Fargo placed his hand on his Colt and a sneer on his face. "Look who it is."

Robert Shanks was impeccably dressed, as always, including his cane. He leaned on it and grinned. "You look as if you're ready to shoot me."

"It would serve you right," Fargo said.

"You're still mad about my offer?"

"Don't play me for a jackass."

Shanks motioned at Clyburn and Jareck and the rest of his protectors. "You might get me but you won't get all of them before they drop you."

"Where did you bury the body?"

Shanks gave a start. "I'm here because one of my men told me you stopped by to see me. Something about McCullock being dead. Are you accusing me?"

"I sure as hell am."

"You're serious?"

"Do I look like I'm joking, you son of a bitch?"

Shanks flushed with anger. "I tell you, I had nothing to do with it." He paused. "How did he die, anyway?"

"As if you don't know," Fargo retorted. "He was knifed. Probably in the back."

"Why probably?"

"All we found was part of his shirt. He's disappeared, like so many others you wanted out of the way."

"I won't deny I wanted his claim but I had no part in this. I swear to you on my mother's grave."

"I doubt you had a mother."

"For once I'm being honest."

Fargo slid his thumb around the Colt's hammer. "As for the claim, you'll get your hands on it over my dead body."

"If he's dead I can file on it like anyone else."

"Someone else already has legal claim."

"Who?"

Fargo grinned. "Mac left it to me in his will." Reaching into his shirt with his other hand, he drew out the document. "Read it and weep, you bastard."

Shanks unfolded the papers and scanned the first page. He flipped to the last and said more to himself than to Fargo, "Clever of the old goat. I'll give him that. Hardly anyone ever thinks of a will." He folded it and handed it back.

"That's it?" Fargo said. "You're not going to rip it up?"

"What good would that do? Wills have to be registered, and that means your name is now on the claim. I'm not a simpleton, Fargo. I know the legalities almost as well as any lawyer."

Fargo hid his disappointment. He'd hoped that Shanks would fly into a rage and give him an excuse to gun him down.

But the lord of Tarryall was thoughtfully tapping his cane. "I need to rethink things. And again, I didn't have anything to do with McCullock vanishing." He wheeled and walked off with his six-gun entourage.

All but one.

Clyburn didn't move. He stood with a thumb wedged close to his belt buckle.

"You want something?" Fargo snapped.

"He's telling you the truth."

"Like hell."

The shooter shrugged. "I have no stake in this. And I'd know if Shanks gave the order to make your friend disappear."

A sliver of doubt punctured Fargo's fury.

"Shanks was serious about waiting you out. He kept laughing about it, and saying how he couldn't wait to go see McCullock after you were gone."

"Why are you telling me this?"

Clyburn shrugged. "Call it professional courtesy. You're one of the few men I've ever met that I respect."

"Should I break out a violin?"

Clyburn chuckled. "Hard as nails. But it seems to me you're letting your hate get the better of you."

"You're trying to stop me from blowing out your boss's wick."

"Think for a minute," Clyburn said. "If it wasn't Shanks it had to be someone else."

"No one else was after McCullock's claim."

"But someone is after you. Those farmers you told us about. Maybe they killed him to spite you."

Fargo hadn't thought of that. And it just might be. They'd killed two Arapahos for no other reason than their skin was red and not white.

Clyburn turned to go. "Better watch your back from here on out."

"From them or you?"

Stopping, Clyburn shook his head. "How many times do I have to tell you? With me it won't be in the back. Mr. Shanks says to gun you, I'll come at you head-on."

Fargo believed him.

"But the others, now, Jareck and the rest, they don't have . . ." Clyburn stopped for a moment. "I reckon you'd call it honor. They'd as soon shoot you in the back as the front. Hell, they'd prefer the back so there's no chance of you shooting them." Clyburn paused. "And once Mr. Shanks has time to ponder, once he sees that he can't wait you out, he'll choose another way. If you follow my drift." He strolled away.

Fargo stood thinking, then climbed on the Ovaro. He reined to the street and looked both ways. He made sure to scan the rooftops.

Only one horse was at the hitch rail in front of the Stopover. Fargo tied off the stallion and went in. The office door was open and Marian was at her desk. For once she wasn't scribbling in her ledgers. She had a mirror propped on her desk and was fluffing her hair with a brush.

She saw him and smiled.

"This blamed wind. It plays havoc with a girl's appearance."

Fargo sat on the edge of the desk. "I came by to see you earlier."

"What's on your mind?" she asked without looking up from the mirror.

"I thought you might like to help me celebrate."

Marian swiped the brush at a tangle above her ear. "Is it your birthday?"

"I'm the new owner of a gold claim."

"Jim McCullock and you both have one? Is yours anywhere near his?"

Fargo frowned at his lapse. He should have told her about McCullock straight off. They knew each other, although they weren't close friends. "Jim has disappeared."

Marian's head jerked up, the brush poised. "Not him too?"

Fargo nodded. "A lawyer named Finch paid me a visit. Mac made out a will with me as his beneficiary."

"You don't say," Marian said, but she didn't sound excited.

"Something the matter?"

"McCullock has been missing how long?"

"Since this morning."

"He's vanished and might be dead," Marian said, "and you want to celebrate?"

Fargo stood. "You'd rather have me bawl my brains out?"

"Some sorrow would be nice, yes. Just a little to show you cared."

"Go to hell," Fargo said, and stalked out. He was almost to the Ovaro when she caught up and placed her hand on his arm.

"I apologize. That was uncalled for. I know he was your friend, and he thought highly of you."

Fargo grunted and turned to mount.

"I said I'm sorry, you big lunk. Don't go riding off in a huff."

"I don't do huffs," Fargo growled.

"Oh really? And yes, I'll go out with you tonight. So long as it's not to the Dunbar." Marian touched his cheek. "You must be hurting inside."

"Eight o'clock?" Fargo relented.

Marian nodded and kissed him on the cheek and whisked into the Stopover.

Fargo gripped the saddle horn to climb on. Belatedly, he registered a rush of footsteps and spun.

Alonzo was almost on top of him, a knife raised to bury in his back.

19

Fargo was almost caught flat-footed. He didn't expect to be attacked in broad daylight unless it was with a rifle from a distance. He dodged and the blade struck his saddle and caused the Ovaro to shy.

"Bastard!" Alonzo hissed, and came at him again.

Fargo was retreating to gain room. He flashed his hand to his Colt but as he drew his left boot heel came down on a rock and he stumbled. Before he could recover Alonzo was on him. He grabbed Alonzo's knife wrist and Alonzo grabbed his gun wrist. A fierce struggle ensued with each of them seeking to break the other's hold.

Fargo couldn't remember if there had been any passersby in the street. Not that they were likely to lend a hand. In a lawless town like Tarryall people didn't just look the other way when they saw a crime, they ran the other way.

"You killed Milton and Rafer!" Alonzo raged, fire in his eyes.

Fargo hooked a boot behind Alonzo's leg and twisted, seeking to trip him, but Alonzo agilely hopped over his boot. Farmwork had made Alonzo stronger than he looked, and his blade inched toward Fargo's chest. The tip nicked his buckskin shirt.

With a powerful heave, Fargo almost cast him off. But Alonzo held on and they struggled anew.

Turning and twisting, Fargo kicked at Alonzo's knee. Alonzo sidestepped, and drove his boot up and in.

Pain exploded up and down Fargo's leg and he nearly buckled.

Their thrashing carried them into the fence. Flimsy as could be, it buckled, the wood splintering to bits.

Unbalanced, both of them fell. Fargo wound up on the bottom. Seizing his chance, Alonzo bore down with all his weight.

Fargo strained every muscle in his shoulders to push him back. Alonzo hissed, spittle flecking his mouth and dribbling onto Fargo's face.

Something poked hard into Fargo's back. A jagged piece of fence, he figured. The pain made him grit his teeth. He shifted to try to lessen the hurt, and his grip on Alonzo's wrist slipped. Suddenly Alonzo's knife scraped his neck. Instinctively, he heaved up and succeeded in rolling over. But he couldn't cast off Alonzo.

The farmer was practically rabid in his thirst for vengeance.

They rolled once. They rolled twice. The dust of the street was under them. Fargo tasted it in his mouth, in his nose. He rammed his knee at Alonzo's gut but Alonzo avoided the blow and retaliated. Fargo shifted but Alonzo's knee caught him and his stomach flared with torment.

Then Alonzo was on top of him again, and the knife was descending.

Fargo was about to buck when something arced in the air above Alonzo's head. There was a metallic *thwang*, and Alonzo cried out. Again there was a blur of movement, and this time Fargo saw the flat of a shovel connect with the side of Alonzo's head. Blood sprayed from around the tufts of hair poking from Alonzo's ear, and Alonzo groaned and collapsed.

Fargo pushed him off and rose to his feet. He was breathing heavily and covered with dust and dirt. "I'll be damned," he said.

Marian Hatcher was breathing heavily, too. She had a shovel in her hands and was standing over Alonzo, ready to bash him again, if need be. She glanced at him and sheepishly grinned. "I looked out my window and saw you two fighting and ran out to help." She shook the shovel. "This was leaning against the wall by the flower bed so I grabbed it. Did I do good?"

Fargo kissed her. "You did right fine, gorgeous."

Marian blushed. "I've never hit anyone before," she said in some amazement at her audacity.

"You can hit him a few more times if you want," Fargo suggested. "Break a few bones while you're at it."

"You wouldn't really want me to do that."

Little did she know, Fargo reflected. He holstered his Colt and bent and picked up Alonzo's knife and stuck it under his belt.

"This is another of those farmers, I gather?" Marian said. "What will you do with him?"

"Take him to Mac's place. There are a few questions I need to ask."

"You won't hurt him, will you? I feel sort of responsible, hitting him like I did."

"I won't hurt him much," was as far as Fargo would say. Bending, he slid his hands under Alonzo's arms and half carried, half dragged him to the Ovaro. Using his rope, he bound the man's wrists and ankles, then heaved him over the saddle, belly down.

Marian watched intently. "Remember, you can't take the law into your own hands."

"What law?" Fargo said.

"Granted, we don't have a marshal. But you know what I mean. You can't stoop to their level."

"Sure I can."

"But that's wrong, don't you see?"

"If someone kicks me in the teeth, I kick them back," Fargo said. "Only harder."

"You can't set yourself up as judge and hangman," Marian argued. "Why, if everyone did that, where would we all be?"

"There would be a lot less Robert Shanks in this world," Fargo said, and left her staring after him in dismay.

The Ovaro's burden drew more than a few stares but not one person stopped him to ask why he had a trussed-up man over his saddle.

At the shack he grabbed the back of Alonzo's shirt and dumped him. The farmer had been unconscious the whole way back but the shock of slamming to the ground caused him to stir and jerk and then open his eyes and look groggily about. "What? Where?"

"You don't recollect trying to kill me?" Bending, Fargo grabbed his legs and dragged him up and into the shack.

Alonzo hit his head and cried out and cursed. When

Fargo let go, his eyes were bright and clear and filled with rage. "Where am I? What in hell do you think you're doin'?"

Fargo sat at the table and propped his boots on it. "We're having a little talk."

"I'm not sayin' a damn thing to you."

"Where are they?"

"Who?" Alonzo pretended not to understand.

"Willard and the other one. What was his name again?" Fargo had to think about it. "Elias."

"I'm not sayin' a thing."

"Willard tried to shoot me with a rifle, didn't he?"

"He almost nailed you, too. I saw the—" Alonzo stopped and swore and struggled against the ropes. "You ain't got no right, I tell you."

"I had to kill four Arapahos because of you and your friends."

Alonzo stopped struggling. "How's that again?"

"The Arapahos thought I was one of you and tracked me down and almost did me in."

"You don't say," Alonzo said, and laughed. "Too bad they didn't."

"I wasn't sure I'd find the five of you again and then I ran into Rafer."

"And killed him," Alonzo snarled. "And killed Milton, too. But we'll get you. We took a pact, Willard and Elias and me. We're not goin' to rest until one of us feeds you to the worms."

"That's only fair," Fargo said.

"How do you figure?"

"It's fair because I'm not resting until all three of you get what's coming to you."

"So now what?" Alonzo asked, and he couldn't keep a trace of fear out of his voice. "You pull your smoke wagon and blow my brains out?"

"I thought I'd keep you around a while," Fargo said. "As a pet."

"The hell you say."

"I might ask a barkeep or two to spread the word that I have you. By tomorrow it will be all over town."

"What good would that do?" Alonzo demanded. He gave a start and glanced at the door and answered his own question. "Wait. I get it. You're fixin' to use me as bait. Keep me here and wait for Willard and Elias to come after me."

Fargo grinned.

"It won't work," Alonzo said. "They're too smart to fall for a trick like that."

"When it comes to brains," Fargo said, "neither struck me as having any to spare."

"Willard does. And Elias is real cautious. They won't come walkin' in here for you to blast to kingdom come."

"We'll see."

Alonzo gnashed his teeth. "All this over a couple of stinkin' redskins. Redskins you didn't even know."

"I've lived with Indians now and then," Fargo informed him.

Alonzo nodded. "I thought as much. Explains why you're an Injun lover. All the scalpin' and killin' Injuns do to white folks and you side with them against your own skin."

"It's not the skin," Fargo said. "It's the people under the skin."

"You're sayin' that Injuns ain't no different than us? Mister, you are loco as hell. Red ain't white and white ain't red."

"And hate is hate," Fargo said.

"You're one of those do-goods—is that it?" Alonzo said in contempt. "You go around imposin' what you think is right on those who don't think the same as you do. What gives you the right?"

"You and your friends tied me. Your friend Rafer stomped on me. You left me lying in the middle of the prairie."

"We left you breathin'. And besides, you started it, you with your redskin airs."

Fargo got up and walked to the door.

"Hold on," Alonzo said. "Where are you off to? You're not goin' to leave me hog-tied here like this, are you?"

"I'm getting my rifle," Fargo said. It just hit him. "If you were watching the other night when Willard had his turn, then it stands to reason Willard and Elias were watching when you jumped me at the Stopover."

Alonzo stiffened.

"I thought so," Fargo said. "I don't need to spread the word. They know I have you. And as soon as it's dark, they'll make their move."

"You think you're so smart," Alonzo said. "But you'll be deader than hell before too long."

20

The lamp was turned low so most of the shack was in shadow. Alonzo lay in the center of the floor, gagged now, as well as bound. The front door was shut and a broom propped against it—not to keep the door from opening, but so that it would fall to the floor when the door was opened, and give warning. The burlap covering the window was tied so no one could peek in.

In a far corner, Fargo sat with the Henry across his legs, waiting with the patience of an Apache. He could sit there all night long, if need be.

The sun had set an hour and a half ago. It was cooler in the shack. From out in the street there came the occasional clomp of hooves as a rider went past or the clatter and rattle of a buckboard.

Fargo was disappointed that Willard and Elias hadn't showed yet. He wanted it over. He wanted it settled.

It could be they were going to wait until they reckoned he was asleep. Which meant it would be hours more.

Alonzo glared.

Fargo could see his eyes, shiny with hate. He'd warned him not to move and so far Alonzo had listened.

Some riders went by, their hoofbeats like the dull pounding of drums.

Fargo shifted to relieve a slight cramp in his lower back. He was hungry and thirsty but he suppressed both.

He wasn't budging. Not until this was done.

Alonzo shifted and grunted and muttered something through his gag.

"Not a peep," Fargo quietly warned.

Down the street a woman laughed. Farther off an infant commenced to squall.

Fargo glanced at the lamp. He hadn't checked the whale oil to see if there was enough to last the night. It wouldn't do to have it go out and leave the room in darkness. He needed to be able to see them when they came.

Rising, he leaned the Henry against the corner and went to the table. As he was bending over the lamp he heard a scrape from outside.

Alonzo heard it, too, and swiveled on his hip toward the door.

There were footsteps, and a hand gripped the outer latch.

Fargo whirled, clearing the Colt and thumbing back the hammer. Already the door was opening, and the broom fell with a *clack*. His finger was around the trigger and he was about to squeeze when an hourglass figure filled the doorway.

"What in the world?" Marian Hatcher blurted, gaping at Alonzo. She had on a dark blue dress and a light blue shawl over her shoulders, and a large purse in her left hand.

Fargo darted over, took her wrist, and pulled her inside. He quickly closed the door and moved over by the table. "What are you doing here?"

"Did you forget we had a supper date?" Marian asked, sounding hurt.

Fargo wanted to kick himself.

"When you didn't show up, I became worried. The last I saw of you, you were hauling this poor man off, remember? I was worried maybe he had gotten loose or his friends had shown up."

"I'm expecting them," Fargo said. "It's not safe here. You have to get out."

Marian stared at Alonzo. "I see. He's the worm and they're the fish." She gave Fargo a sad look. "You're as devious as Shanks."

"You really must skedaddle," Fargo urged, and tried to steer her out but she dug in her heels.

"Not so fast. I can't say as I like this side of you very much. I didn't take you for a coldhearted killer."

"You're forgetting they're out to kill me," Fargo reminded her, his ears cocked for sounds outside.

"I know. But most men would avoid a fight. They would do whatever it took not to shed blood."

"And they would be dead," Fargo said.

"You could ride out," Marian proposed. "Get on your horse and go and that would be the end of it."

"Run away, you mean."

"I call it common sense." Marian put her hand on his arm. "I don't want anything to happen to you. Is that so wrong?"

"I can't," Fargo said.

"Why not? You'll let your foolish male pride get you killed?"

"Male pride, hell. Females have just as much as men do."

"Then why in God's name not?"

Fargo had never put it into words before but he did the best he could. "I need to be able to look at myself in the mirror. I need to be able to live with myself day in and day out."

"Then it is pride."

"No," Fargo said. "It's about not being yellow. It's about standing up for myself. It's about doing what's right even if everyone else thinks it's wrong."

"I'm sorry. I just don't understand. You have nothing to prove. You've already demonstrated you have grit to spare."

"I run off now," Fargo said, "I'll run off again some day. I can't have that."

"Living is better than dying."

"Not if it's living as a coward. Not if it's letting other men ride roughshod."

"We can argue until doomsday and I won't change my mind."

Fargo saw Alonzo raise his head and look at the front door.

"I'll grant you that we all have to be true to our natures," Marian went on. "But not at the expense of human life. We are all of us—" She got no further.

Fargo pressed a hand to her mouth to shut her up and gestured at the latch.

It was slowly turning.

Fargo pulled Marian toward the corner but they had taken only a couple of steps when the door flew inward. Willard burst inside, his rifle level at his hip.

Fargo dived, pulling Marian with him, afraid she would take lead. He snapped off a shot but missed and hit the jamb.

Willard fired at almost the same instant. But not at them. He shot at the lamp and it erupted in a shower of flame. In a twinkling the shack was plunged in Stygian black.

Lying on his side on the floor, Marian close behind him, Fargo strained to see. The flash had temporarily blinded him. He was aware of sounds, of scuffing and an oath, and of vague moving figures. He was worried for Marian's sake that more lead would be thrown at them but no gunshots rang out.

Silence fell.

Suddenly Fargo's vision cleared. Even in the gloom he could tell that the door was wide-open, and that Alonzo was gone. "Stay here," he said, and was on his feet and outside in a few bounds.

The Ovaro was where he had left it. Otherwise the yard was empty.

Fargo sprinted to the street.

A pair of riders had heard the shots and drawn rein and were staring. Across the way a woman in a bonnet, with two small children clutched to her legs, was frozen in fear.

"Three men," Fargo said to the riders. "Which way did they go?"

One of the riders pointed.

Fargo gave chase. They couldn't have gone far. He would catch them and it would be over. But he went a block and didn't spot them and another block and still nothing and he stopped. They could have ducked between any of the shacks and cabins he'd passed. He ran back, searching for any sign of them, but it was futile.

Marian hadn't listened. She was in front of McCullock's, her arms across her bosom. "They got away?"

Fargo nodded.

"It's just as well. Maybe they've had enough. Maybe they'll take their friend and forget about this silly vendetta and leave Tarryall."

"Wishful thinking," Fargo said. He slid a cartridge from a belt loop to replace the empty in the cylinder.

The riders had moved on and the woman with the children had gone away.

"If you want the truth, I'm glad they fled," Marian said. "I'm happy no blood was spilled."

Fargo held his tongue. She was one of those who thought everyone was like she was and always had the best of intentions. She saw only what she wanted to see.

"Nothing to say?" Marian challenged him.

"Not that you'd agree with."

They went inside. The place reeked of smoke and burnt oil. There had been only the one lamp and it was in pieces.

"You were lucky this place didn't catch on fire," Marian told him.

Fargo holstered the Colt and claimed the Henry. "Do you still want to eat?"

"Do you still want to take me? I get the impression you're mad at me."

"I'm not mad at all," Fargo said. Angry, yes, but he couldn't hold her good intentions against her.

"Then yes, I'm famished. Where would you like to eat?"

Fargo ushered her out. "You know the town better than me. You pick."

It was called Edna's Kitchen and a sign out front stated that it was open from six a.m. until midnight six days a week but closed on the Sabbath and had "the best home-cooked meals this side of the Divide."

Fargo was skeptical, especially since the cook was a man in a dirty apron. The menu had buffalo, which was unusual that high up in the mountains. He ordered it, thinking he'd be served days-old meat not fit for a dog.

He was pleasantly surprised. The buff steak was fresh and thick and the trimmings were hot and delicious.

Marian had potpie. A lot of women would have been ruffled by the incident at the shack but it hadn't dampened her spirits or her appetite. She chatted gaily about her parents, who were back in Indiana, and a sister who was married and settled down.

Fargo let her ramble. The more she talked, the less he had to. He was thinking about where he would sleep for the night when Marian cleared her throat and gave him his answer.

"I baked a pie earlier. How would you like to come to my house for dessert?"

"What will the neighbors think?"

"We'll sneak in," Marian said, and laughed. "What do you say? Do you like the idea?"

Fargo imagined the luscious charms her dress concealed. "I like it a lot."

21

They rode double as they had to Edna's. Marian rested her cheek on his shoulder and wrapped her arms around his waist.

The night was cool and peaceful and Fargo hoped it stayed that way. Willard and Elias and Alonzo were still out there and would undoubtedly jump him again. He had to do something about it but it could wait until morning.

At that, Fargo grinned. He could feel Marian's breasts against his back. The pressure set his groin to twitching. Now and then her breath fluttered on his neck and sent a warm sensation down his back.

At her house Fargo rode around to the rear and tied the Ovaro.

Marian unlocked the back door and lit a lamp in the kitchen. As the glow spread she draped her shawl over the back of a chair and tossed her purse onto the counter. "Have a seat. I'll have that pie ready in no time."

"No hurry," Fargo said. Perching, he watched her putter about and undressed her with his eyes. He was hungry, but not for food.

"It's been a long day for you, hasn't it?" Marian made small talk.

"It'll be longer," Fargo said.

She got the pie from the pantry and set it on the counter. Opening a drawer, she drew out a long knife. "I hope you like apple."

"There's only one thing I like to eat more."

Marian looked over her shoulder. "And what would that be?"

Fargo stared at her, low down.

"Oh my," Marian said softly, and blushed. "You come

right out with it, don't you?" She coughed and commenced to slice.

"I can see why Shanks is interested in you," Faro said.

"Let's not bring him up, shall we?" Marian requested, and slashed at the pie as if stabbing it.

To cover for his blunder, Fargo said, "I'm glad I ran into you."

"I like you, too," Marian said. She scooped a slice of pie onto a plate, got a fork from the same drawer, and brought the plate over. "Here you go." She bent to set it down.

Reaching up, Fargo gently placed his hand at the back of her neck and pulled her face to his. She tensed as if afraid and then their mouths met. He kissed her softly, rimming her lips with his tongue, and let go.

Marian was still holding the pie. She set the plate in front of him and straightened. "What was that for?" she asked huskily.

"My idea of topping on the dessert."

She returned to the counter. "You give a person naughty thoughts."

"Good."

"I've never had a man be so direct," Marian said softly. "Most beat around the bush."

"I plow through them," Fargo said.

"If you were any more forceful, you'd have ripped off my dress by now."

"Dresses cost a woman money."

Marian laughed. "That's terribly considerate of you, kind sir."

"I've got enough in my poke to buy you a new one, though," Fargo said.

Marian glanced at him. "You wouldn't?" she said. Picking up her slice, she came to the table and sat across from him. She didn't meet his gaze but concentrated on her pie. "How does it taste?"

"I haven't found out yet."

Another blush crept from her neckline to her hairline. "You're making me light-headed."

"Good," Fargo said again.

Marian coughed and forked a piece of apple into her mouth and daintily chewed. "Can I ask you something?"

Fargo shrugged. "It's your house."

"How many women have you been with?"

"Anything but that," Fargo said.

"Who was the last lady you were with?"

"Or that," Fargo said.

"I'm only curious," Marian said apologetically. "Believe it or not, I don't do this every day. Nor every month or every six months." She stared across, studying him. "But there is something about you. Something I can't put my finger on."

"As soon as my pants are off, you can."

Marian snorted, and covered her mouth with her hand. "Please. Let me get my pie down before you start devouring me."

"Don't take all night," Fargo said, and smiled.

Marian forked another piece into her mouth. "To change the subject, when will you be going back up into the mountains to work your gold claim?"

"Who says I will?" Fargo said.

Marian stopped chewing. "Jim McCullock did you a tremendous kindness."

"You think so?"

"What are you saying? If someone left me a gold claim, I'd be happy as could be."

"I'll be happy later," Fargo said. "First I have to live out the week."

"Oh, you mean Shanks."

"McCullock didn't do it out of the goodness of his heart. He did it so that if anything happened to him, I'd have to kill Shanks or be killed."

"McCullock wanted revenge from beyond the grave?"

"More or less," Fargo said.

"I don't believe it. I didn't know McCullock all that well but the impression I had was that he wasn't that kind of man."

Fargo didn't argue. It was easy for her to defend McCullock; she wasn't in Shanks's gun sights. He finished his pie and pushed the plate back.

Marian was still picking at hers. She noticed him looking at her and asked, "You're not in any hurry, are you?"

"We have all night."

"You realize, don't you, that if Shanks finds out about us,

and what we're contemplating doing, he'll want you dead more than ever."

"You're worth it."

"What a sweet thing to say."

Fargo didn't mention that he was going after Shanks anyway, that despite what Shanks and Clyburn had told him he still suspected it was Shanks, and not the farmers, who had a hand in McCullock's disappearance.

Marian finally downed the last bite. She took his plate and hers to the sink and set them in it. Covering the pie with a cloth, she carried it into the pantry and came back out and closed the pantry door. "Would you care for some liquor? I'm thinking of having a glass of brandy to loosen me up."

"Whiskey if you have it." Fargo had no objection to her taking as long as she needed. Some women took a while to work into the mood.

The bottles were on the top shelf of a cabinet. She brought two glasses and filled his halfway and hers all of the way. He was amused when she emptied it in a few gulps.

"No need to be so nervous."

"That's easy for you to say." Marian grabbed the brandy bottle and refilled her glass.

Rising, Fargo came around the table. She froze like a rabbit caught in the glare of a lantern and her eyes widened slightly. Cupping her chin, he kissed her lightly on the lips, the cheek, the forehead. She kissed him on the chin and he slowly molded his body to hers as their mouths glued and their tongues entwined.

When they parted, Marian closed her eyes and said dreamily, "Mmmmm. That was nice."

Fargo cupped her bottom and she gasped. A look came over her, a look Fargo had seen before, a look of need. She tried to crawl into his shirt while sucking on his tongue.

Suddenly scooping her into his arms, Fargo said simply, "The bedroom."

"Up the stairs and to the right."

They kissed all the way. Fargo was careful not to bump her against the banister or the bedroom door. The bed was covered with a quilt. He laid her down but she said, "Hold on," and got back up and pulled the quilt down.

"This was my grandmother's," she explained. "I don't want anything to happen to it." She gave his spurs a pointed look.

Fargo sat and removed them, and his boots, as well. He added his gun belt to the pile and turned.

Marian just sat there, her hands in her lap, waiting.

"Sometimes the women take their own clothes off," Fargo mentioned.

"Oh. Sorry. I told you. I don't have a lot of experience."

She would, Fargo reflected, before morning came. He had her shift so her back was to him and pried at a row of tiny buttons.

"I feel I should be doing something," Marian said.

"Keep this warm, then," Fargo said, and taking her hand, he brought it behind her and placed it on his manhood.

"My goodness," Marian bleated.

Fargo went on prying. Tiny buttons were a peeve of his and he had half a mind to draw his toothpick and peel the dress like a banana. Instead he went on undoing them until the dress loosened and slid down around her shoulders. Her hand hadn't moved the entire time.

Turning her so she faced him, he eased her dress lower, exposing a white chemise. He drank in the sight of the full swell of her breasts, and her nipples.

"I know I'm not that good-looking—" Marian said, apparently mistaking his appreciation for hesitation.

"You're a sight for any man's eyes," Fargo said. Covering both mounds, he squeezed. Marian arched and her mouth parted and she uttered a low moan. His mouth found hers and he kissed and squeezed and pinched. Her kisses became hotter, her nipples became nails. Lowering the chemise, he inhaled her right nipple and flicked it with his tongue. She cooed and ran her hand through his hair, knocking his hat off.

Fargo eased her onto the bed and stretched out beside her. He pulled at her dress and she helped by raising her bottom so he could get it all the way off. Tossing it to the floor next to his hat, he ran a hand over her soft cotton chemise from the top hem to the junction of her thighs.

Marian trembled and her eyes became hooded with lust.

"I have never wanted a man as much as I want you," she whispered.

"Show me," Fargo teased.

Marian reached up to pull him close, and froze.

So did Fargo.

From downstairs had come a loud creak.

22

Fargo was off the bed and in a crouch with the Colt in his hand before the sound faded. "Was that one of your doors?"

"No," Marian said. "It's the window in the parlor. I've been meaning to fix it but I just never got around to it."

"Stay here." Fargo glided to the door and glanced back. "And this time, do as I tell you." He slid out and moved down the hall to the top of a stairs.

A shadow moved in the parlor.

Staying low, Fargo took each step slowly, placing his weight with care so the stair wouldn't creak as the window had done. He was halfway down when the muzzle of a rifle poked into the hall and a few seconds later so did a face.

It was Alonzo. He looked up and down the hall and then did something strange: he pumped the barrel up and down.

A signal, Fargo realized. He heard the front door ease open. He also thought he heard the back door open, as well.

Alonzo nodded at someone at the front of the house and then turned toward the kitchen and nodded again.

All three of them were there.

Fargo mentally swore. Here he was in the open on the stairs with one enemy below and others coming from both directions. He needed to hunt cover. He began to ease up to the landing.

Alonzo sidled out of the parlor and tucked at the knees with his back against the wall.

A shadow moved down the hall from the direction of the front door. Willard crept into view. He didn't have a rifle or a revolver this time; he had a shotgun.

Fargo's mouth went dry. Odds were, the shotgun was loaded with buckshot. And as the saying went, buckshot meant burying. He'd be blown in half if Willard caught him dead center.

Another shadow heralded Elias, anxiously licking his lips.

"No sign of them?" Alonzo whispered.

Elias shook his head.

Willard whispered, "They must be upstairs."

All three looked up.

For a span of heartbeats the tableau froze. Fargo wasn't to the top and they could see his head and shoulders. Their surprise delayed their reactions, and he acted. He banged a shot at Alonzo, spun, and fired at Willards. Neither went down. Alonzo's rifle cracked and so did Elias's even as Willard swung the shotgun.

Fargo took a step and threw himself at the landing. Behind him a cannon went off and the whole house seemed to shake. The wall exploded, showering debris. Fargo scrambled up and pushed to his hands and knees.

The three farmers had disappeared.

Fargo was sure he had hit Alonzo but not so sure about Willard. He waited, coiled, but nothing happened until Elias whispered from near the kitchen.

"Did he get you?"

"Winged me," Alonzo answered from the parlor.

"How bad?" From Willard, in the vicinity of the front door.

"I'll live," Alonzo said.

Fargo knew he shouldn't but he hollered, "Sorry to hear that, you son of a bitch." He regretted it when all three popped out and cut loose. He dropped flat. Slugs struck on either side while above him a hole the size of a watermelon was blown out of the wall.

Fargo reared up to shoot but they had ducked back. He flattened. If he was in their boots, he'd rush the landing all at once, but either they were being cautious or they were up to something because they didn't show themselves.

Something poked Fargo in the back and he nearly jumped.

Marian had his gun belt. "Thought you might need this," she whispered.

Fargo took it and put his mouth to her ear. "I'm obliged. Now get your ass back in the bedroom."

"Is that the thanks I get?"

Fargo pushed her. He took it for granted she would listen and turned toward the hall and strapped on the belt.

He quickly replaced the spent cartridges, then risked raising his head high enough to peer over.

Silence prevailed.

No shadows moved anywhere.

Fargo started down the stairs on his belly. He saw more and more of the hall until near the bottom he could see that the hall was empty and the front door was open. Rising, he glanced around at the kitchen. The back door was wide-open too.

Darting into the parlor, Fargo saw that it was empty and the window was up. Red drops led to it. He ran over and warily stuck his head out. There were clumps of grass and nothing else.

Fargo turned and nearly collided with Marian Hatcher, who had a blanket over her shoulders. "You don't listen worth a damn."

"I was worried about you."

"Go back upstairs." Fargo went around her and down the hall to the front door. The yard was empty. He closed the door and threw the bolt and turned, and almost bumped into her again. "Damn it to hell, woman."

"You sure do cuss a lot."

Fargo pushed her ahead of him to the stairs. "Go on up," he said, and swatted her on the fanny. He kept on going, through the kitchen.

The Ovaro, thank God, was still there.

Fargo slammed the door and worked the bolt and started to turn but stopped. "You're behind me, aren't you?"

"I told you I was worried."

Sighing, Fargo faced her and shoved the Colt into his holster.

"Why are you so angry?"

"What if they'd shot me?"

"You'd protect me."

"Ever hear of a stray bullet?" As Fargo was well aware, when men got to swapping lead, bystanders were as likely to take slugs as the men doing the swapping. It was why anyone who spent a lot of time in saloons hit the floor when a shot rang out.

"I know how to duck," Marian said.

"You're too damn stubborn," Fargo said.

"I can't help how I feel."

Fargo didn't like the sound of that. "You feel like you want to be shot?"

"Don't be ridiculous. I was talking about my feelings for you."

"You're not making more of this than there is?"

"Never."

Fargo had his doubts. But he didn't press the issue. He needed to get her back in the mood and an argument wasn't the way to do it.

Grunting, Fargo wedged a kitchen chair against the door as added insurance. She was waiting by the table. He turned the lamp all the way down and she started to walk off but he clasped her hand and pulled her to him. She had pulled her dress up to her shoulders but hadn't done the buttons up so it was a simple matter for him to slide it down again, all the way to her waist.

"What are you doing?"

"What does it look like?" Fargo pressed against her, his right hand on a breast, his left delving down.

"Shouldn't we go upstairs?" Marian suggested, her breath heavy with rekindled yearning.

"What for?"

"There's a bed."

Fargo nodded behind her. "There's a table."

"But won't that be uncomfortable?"

"Let's find out."

Fargo slid his left hand around her bottom and easily boosted her up. She parted her mouth and her legs. He fastened his mouth to the former and ground roughly against the latter and she uttered a tiny whine. Gradually her body loosened and she grew as warm as she had been in the bedroom. Her mouth became molten. For someone who didn't have a lot of experience, she was suddenly doing things to excite him that even experienced ladies seldom did. Her hands, her mouth, were everywhere.

Soon there were discarded clothes all around their feet. When her last article was cast aside, Fargo took a half step back to admire her beauty. Disheveled hair cascaded over her shoulders, hunger glistened in her luminous eyes, and her lips were red and full. Her breasts were ripe fruit, her nipples begging him to bite them. The flat of her belly, the sweep of her silken thighs, were the icing on the carnal cake.

Fargo kissed, licked, caressed, and rubbed. She did all that he did, and then some. She was fond of sucking on his earlobes and liked to swirl her tongue in circles around and around his neck.

Eventually, Fargo judged she was ready. He aligned his pole and pulled her forward a little and was in her sheath in a quick upward thrust. She cried out and clutched him.

He eased her down and forward so there was room for his knees. The hard wood stung a little but he didn't care. The pleasure eclipsed the pain.

It was a sturdy table. It had to be. He plunged and plunged and she wrapped her legs fast and sought to suck him into her mouth. Her sheath was wet velvet. The table shook and she shook and after a while she arched her back and spurted and he gripped her hips and rode her like a bronc.

Marian coasted to a limp stop and lay still, apparently thinking it was over.

Fargo disabused her of the notion with harder and faster strokes. She looked up, wide-eyed, and tried to match the ferocity of his need. The table's legs were swaying like reeds in a storm when she nipped his ear and it triggered the deluge he had been holding back.

There was nothing like the feeling. Not whiskey, as much as he liked a good drink. Not cards, as much as he liked poker. Not even, if he was honest with himself, a brilliant sunrise on a mountain. He'd once heard someone say that this was what made the world go round, and they sure as hell were right.

In time he slowed and lay on her, slick with sweat and tingling from his release. He was content to stay there a while but she shifted under him and complained that it was uncomfortable so he slid off, grabbed his gun belt and his clothes, and followed her upstairs. She was carrying her clothes and nearly tripped over her dress going up.

Fargo sank onto the bed and into a sleep so deep he wouldn't have woke if the house fell down around him.

His habit was to rouse at the crack of dawn but for a rare instance his habit failed him. He knew when his eyes opened that, judging by the sunlight streaming in the window, it was the middle of the morning.

Fargo was flat on his back, Marian on her side. He sluggishly raised his head and was jarred to his full senses by what he saw.

Jareck was in the doorway.

23

Jareck was leaning against the jamb and his thumbs were hooked in his gun belt. "Mornin', bare ass," he said, and smirked. "Bet you weren't expectin' company."

Fargo tried to remember where he had dropped his gun belt.

"Ain't she a sight," Jareck said, running his gaze over Marian. "The boss would give anything to see her in the altogether. I'll have to dress her when I'm done. He finds out I saw her naked, he'll skin me alive."

Fargo remembered. His gun belt was on the floor, midway down the bed. He gauged the distance.

"No, you don't," Jareck said, and just like that his Smith & Wesson was in his hand. "I hear you're fast but you're not faster than a bullet."

Fargo settled back, his every muscle tense. "I could use my pants."

"I bet you could," Jareck said. "They're lyin' over here on the floor. Want me to fetch them for you?" He laughed coldly.

Fargo looked past him. "Where are the rest?"

"Clyburn and the others?" Jareck grinned. "It's just me."

"Shanks sent you?" Fargo would have thought he rated the whole pack.

"You're not payin' attention," Jareck said. "I just got done tellin' you that if he found out I was here, he'd skin me alive."

"He didn't send you?"

"God Almighty, I didn't take you for stupid," Jareck said. "Wake the hell up."

Marian stirred and murmured.

"Might as well wake her up while you're at it," Jareck said. "She should see it comin', the bitch."

"See what?" Fargo said.

"Maybe you *are* stupid," Jareck said, and wiggled the Smith & Wesson. "What do you think?"

"You're going to shoot us?"

"The light dawns."

Fargo put his hands flat on the bed. "I can savvy me. But what will Shanks say about blowing out her wick?"

"Not me," Jareck said. "You."

"You're going to kill her and fix it so I get the blame?"

"You're slow but you get there," Jareck said. "I'll gun her with yours and then do you and everyone will figure you shot her and shot yourself out of remorse or whatever the hell they call it."

"And you're doing this on your own?"

Jareck glowered and took a step into the bedroom. "How many times do I have to say the same damn thing? Shanks doesn't know I'm here. Clyburn doesn't know I'm here. No one does. I snuck off before they were awake."

Fargo tightened his legs and arm muscles. "Why kill her when Shanks wouldn't want you to?"

Jareck took another step. "Haven't you ever heard of two birds with one stone?"

"He cares for her." Fargo stalled.

"Hell, mister. Robert Shanks doesn't give a damn about anyone but himself. He doesn't love her. He wants to poke her, is all. When a woman says no it drives him loco. No one can ever say no to him. Sayin' no is like wavin' a red blanket in front of a bull. He'll go after it with all he has."

"I still don't savvy," Fargo said. "Why do you want her dead?"

"So Shanks will be himself again. I'm sick of him moonin' over her. He thinks she's pure as the driven snow and even wants to marry her." Jareck laughed and shook his head. "If he could only see the bitch now."

Marian chose that moment to roll over toward Fargo and curl on her side. She muttered something and smacked her lips and was still.

"Look at the stupid cow," Jareck said. "Doesn't even know I'm here."

Out of the corner of his eye, Fargo saw Marian's eyelids crack open.

"He'll get over her," Jareck was saying. "I'm doin' him a favor by snuffin' her. And a second favor by killin' you. Now he can get his hands on that claim of yours."

Fargo saw Marian look at him. He gave a barely perceptible nod and opened his mouth wide as if he were yawning.

Marian blinked twice to show she understood.

"Am I borin' you?" Jareck asked.

"One of us is stupid and it's not me," Fargo said. "Shanks will never believe I killed her."

"Who knows what anybody will do?" Jareck said, and smiled. "Time to get this over with."

"I agree," Fargo said, and glanced at Marian, who opened her mouth wide and let out with a piercing shriek.

Jareck swung toward her, startled.

Which was exactly what Fargo hoped he would do. Launching himself over the side of the bed, Fargo dived for the Colt. Jareck's revolver crashed but whether Jareck had shot at him or Marian, Fargo didn't know. His outstretched hand closed on the Colt and he yanked it from the holster and rolled toward the wall. He glimpsed Jareck coming around the end of the bed and snapped off a shot that rocked the gun shark on his boot heels.

Jareck fired, the slug biting into the wood a hand's-width from Fargo's face.

Fargo thumbed back the hammer and slammed a second slug to Jareck's torso.

Reeling, his arms moving in small circles, Jareck said, "No, no, no." He tried to steady his gun hand.

Fargo shot him between the eyes.

Gore and hair splattered the ceiling and the killer melted where he stood.

With the acrid sting of gun smoke in his nose, Fargo heaved onto the bed. "Are you—?" he said, and stopped.

Marian had her hand over her mouth and nose and commenced to cough. "Did I do all right?" she asked.

Fargo smiled. "You did fine." He slid off and grabbed his gun belt and his clothes. "I'll be right back. For once stay put."

He padded downstairs, his bare feet slapping the cool floorboards. He checked the front door. It was still bolted. He checked the back door. It was still bolted. The parlor window was closed but another window in a small room between the parlor and kitchen wasn't and explained how Jareck got in. He slammed it down and went to the kitchen.

In short order Fargo was dressed. He strapped his gun belt around his waist and remembered to replace the spent cartridge. After kindling the stove he put coffee on to perk and went back upstairs.

Marian was still in bed, the blanket pulled to her chin.

"You're not dressed?"

"You told me to stay put."

"Now you listen?" Fargo said, and laughed.

"Would you do me a favor and get his body out of here? I don't care to look at it."

"Squeamish?"

"About bodies not so much. About brains and blood all over, yes, I'm afraid I am."

Fargo hauled the mortal remains of Jareck out the back door and concealed the hired gun behind the woodpile for the time being. He went back in and washed his hands. The coffee was about hot enough so he set out two cups.

As he was pouring Marian wandered in. She had put a robe on and was wearing slippers.

"God, I need that," she said. Taking a seat, she sipped, and smiled. "Do you also mop floors?"

"Not if I can help it." Fargo sat across from her.

"Too bad. After we're done I have to clean up the mess in the bedroom."

"You're taking it well."

Marian didn't respond right away. She drank and gazed out the window and sighed. "If you're expecting hysterics, I'm not the type. I made up my mind a long time ago that I wasn't going to be one of those women who scream when she sees a mouse."

"You'll make some man a fine wife some day," Fargo made the mistake of saying.

"And you would make a fine husband," Marian said, her eyes saying even more.

"If I take the body to the undertaker's," Fargo changed the subject, "word might get back to Shanks."

"What else can you do?" Marian asked. "There's no law to speak of, but burying bodies in backyards is generally discouraged."

"I'll think of something."

"Are you hungry? I can fix breakfast."

The mention of food made Fargo's stomach growl. "I wouldn't say no to bacon and eggs."

In twenty minutes he was stuffing himself. Whether to impress him or because she was as hungry as he was, Marian fixed a mountain of scrambled eggs with enough sizzling bacon for four people, and hot biscuits, besides.

Marian finished eating first. She excused herself, saying she had to get ready to go to the Stopover. "I've never been this late before. It's all your fault."

"I don't recollect you pushing me away," Fargo said.

She had the decency to blush, and hurried out.

Fargo sat drinking another cup and dabbing at the bacon grease with a biscuit smeared in butter. Finally he rose and went out to deal with the body.

After the good night's sleep and the meal, he was feeling fine. His good feeling lasted until he got to the woodpile.

Jareck's body wasn't there.

"How in hell?" Fargo blurted. Drag marks showed where someone had dragged the body to the side of the house and apparently hauled it over the fence and out to a side street. There, he lost the trail in a jumble of foot- and hoofprints.

Fargo stood there scratching his head. The only ones he could think of who would take it were Shanks's other leather slappers. But why hadn't they come after him? He walked to the front of the house and scanned the street but they were long gone.

He was almost to the porch when Marian came out looking as radiant as a new bride. "Here you are," she said. "I have to go. You're welcome to stay as long as you want." She pecked him and swished off.

Fargo had plans of his own. He climbed on the Ovaro and rode to Main Street where he visited saloon after saloon, asking the bartenders if they had seen the three farmers. None had, that they could recollect. He asked each barkeep to keep his eyes peeled, and as an inducement he promised twenty dollars if they got word to him at McCullock's shack.

He was coming out of the last saloon when a shadow slipped to his side and a gun muzzle was poked into his ribs.

"We've been looking for you," Clyburn said.

24

Clyburn wasn't alone. Two others came from the right and two more from the left, all with their hands on their six-shooters.

"What can I do for you gents?" Fargo said.

Clyburn grinned. "Got to hand it to you. You have more sand than a desert." He bobbed his head at another of the guns for hire. "Frank, take his smoke wagon. Do it careful. This one is more dangerous than most."

"He can't bite with his teeth pulled," Frank said, and reaching around, he snatched the Colt from Fargo's holster.

"We're taking a walk," Clyburn informed him. "Do exactly as I say and you'll get to where we're going without taking lead." He stepped back and motioned. "Down the steps and to the left. Stay in the middle of the street."

Fargo did as they wanted, for now. "We're not going to the Dunbar Hotel?" The hotel was in the other direction.

Clyburn shook his head. "There's a cabin a few blocks away. Mr. Shanks is waiting to see you."

Fargo sauntered along as if he didn't have a care in the world but his mind worked furiously. If he was going to break away he needed to do it now, while there were a lot of people around.

As if Clyburn had read his thoughts, the man in the black hat barked an order and the other four surrounded him.

"In case you get ideas," Clyburn said.

They went three blocks down and turned right and went another two blocks to a cabin no different from the scores of others. It had a yard but no fence. The front door was open. Four leather slappers were out in front and one of them turned and stuck his head inside and said something and out came Robert Shanks, as dandified as ever, and holding his cane.

"Look who it is," Shanks said icily. To Clyburn he said, "Took you long enough."

"He wasn't at McCullock's," Clyburn replied. "We had to hunt all over."

Shanks flicked his cane and the four men surrounding Fargo stepped back. "You're wondering what this is about, no doubt."

"I want my Colt."

"I'm sure you do," Shanks said, "but I don't care to end up like the man inside." He motioned. "Why don't you have a look?"

"This is your place?"

"Hell, no. The desk clerk at the Dunbar was handed a note." Shanks fished in a pocket and held out a folded piece of paper.

Fargo opened it. Someone had scrawled in pencil, *You can find your man at 214 Tercer. He was shot by Fargo. A friend.* He stepped to the doorway. Jareck's body had been dumped on its back. One leg was bent unnaturally under the other and Jareck's lifeless eyes were fixed on the rafters.

"I want the bastard who did this," Shanks said.

His face impassive, Fargo turned. "Which bastard would that be?"

Shanks took the note. "It had to be one of those farmers you told me about. The desk clerk said it was someone in overalls and a straw hat." He swore. "The damned jackasses. They think they can kill one of my men and set me on you so I kill you for them. How dumb do they think I am?"

"There's a lot of dumb going around," Fargo said.

Shanks motioned. "Take Clyburn, here, and however many of my men you want. Find these hayseeds. I want the sons of bitches dead."

"I swat my own flies," Fargo said.

"Damn it," Shanks said. "No one does this to me and gets away with it."

"Aren't you forgetting something?"

"The gold claim? That can wait." Shanks pointed at the body. "This is more important. What do you say?"

Fargo held out his hand. "My Colt."

"Give it to him," Shanks said sharply.

Clyburn handed it over, his own six-shooter level at his hip, the hammer cocked.

Carefully sliding the Colt into his holster, Fargo remarked, "I'm surprised you'd ask for my help. You run this town. You should be able to find them on your own."

"Don't think I'm not trying," Shanks said. "I have men out asking all over."

Fargo was amused and amazed at how things had worked out. Willard and his friends must have been watching Marian's house and saw him dump the body behind the woodpile. That gave them the idea to take the body and get word to Shanks. And now their little brainstorm was coming back to bite them on the ass.

"Well?" Shanks prompted.

Fargo pretended to mull it over. "I'll take Clyburn."

"No one else?"

"Just him," Fargo said, and walked off to forestall an argument. Spurs jingled and Clyburn caught up but stayed a few steps to one side, out of reach, with his hand on his six-gun. "You're a cautious hombre," Fargo said.

"Live longer that way." Clyburn was regarding him as if he were a rattler coiled to strike. "Why did you pick me?" he asked suspiciously.

"You're the best of his shooters."

"There's more to it."

Fargo reminded himself that Clyburn was smarter than the rest. "You did me a favor when you told me your boss didn't have a hand in McCullock disappearing."

"He didn't," Clyburn said. "But that still doesn't explain the why."

"Go back if you want."

Clyburn frowned. "Can't. Mr. Shanks says I have to work with you, I have to work with you."

Fargo looked at him. "You can relax. I don't back-shoot, either."

After collecting the Ovaro, Fargo returned to Jim McCullock's shack. Clyburn didn't say much and always made it a point to stay well out of arm's reach.

Opening his saddlebags, Fargo took out his coffee. He went inside and put some on to brew. While he waited, he sat at the table.

Clyburn came as far as the doorway.

"There's another chair," Fargo said.

"I'm fine here."

"This will get awful tiresome," Fargo said, "you slinking around."

"It's only until the hayseeds are dealt with," Clyburn said.

"That could take days." Fargo hoped different, but the trio could have been anywhere in Tarryall, or camped outside the town, for all he knew.

Clyburn leaned against the jamb, his right hand never leaving his revolver. "What were you doing visiting all those saloons a while ago?"

"You saw me?"

Clyburn nodded. "We followed you a spell."

Fargo told him.

"That's not a bad idea," Clyburn said. "But the three you're after aren't the only farmers hereabouts."

"Do you have a better idea?"

"As a matter of fact, I do," Clyburn said. "There are only three liveries. How about we pay them a visit and ask if the hayseeds have boarded their horses?"

"A stall and oats costs money," Fargo said. But the more he thought about it as he sat drinking his coffee, the more it appealed to him. The five had come a far piece, all the way from the flatlands of the new state of Kansas. By they time they got to Tarryall, their horses could use rest and feed.

After his third cup Fargo rose. "Lead the way to the closest stable."

"Walk ahead of me," Clyburn said. "I'll give you directions as we go."

Chuckling, Fargo strode out.

One by one they paid a visit to each livery. The response was always the same. The liveryman didn't recall anyone answering to the descriptions Fargo gave, or anyone who had mentioned they were from Kansas.

"It was worth a try," Clyburn said.

Fargo would have liked to go to the Stopover and talk to

Marian, but with Clyburn dogging him, he returned to the shack. He got a deck of cards from his saddlebags, and since Clyburn wouldn't sit down, started playing solitaire.

"That's all you're going to do?" Clyburn asked.

"Unless you have another brainstorm."

"When Mr. Shanks said to look, he didn't mean to sit on your ass."

"I'm open to suggestions."

Clyburn scowled and looked over his shoulder. He suddenly straightened and backed up a few steps into the shack, his body half turned so he always had one eye on Fargo. "You have company."

Fargo set down the cards.

It was Willard. He was cradling the shotgun. He filled the doorway and looked at Fargo. "Before you do anything, lift a finger against me and she dies."

"She?" Clyburn said.

Willard jerked a thumb at Fargo. "He knows who I mean. Don't you, tough man?"

Fargo hid his surprise and a spike of unease. "Marian has no part in this."

"You're fond of her, ain't you?" Willard said with gleeful spite.

"Wait," Clyburn said in confusion. "What's this about Miss Hatcher?"

Willard seemed to grow more confident. "We have her. She's not hurt yet but she will be if you try anything."

"My boss will have your guts," Clyburn said.

"It's his fault we took her," Willard said. "He was supposed to read that note and do Fargo in. That was Alonzo's idea, anyhow. I told him it wouldn't work and it didn't."

"So you took Marian," Fargo said.

Willard nodded. "Here's how it will go. There's a clearing on the east side of the road out of town to the north, about a mile out. At seven we'll be there waiting." He paused. "You don't show up, she dies. You don't come alone, she dies. You give us so much as a lick of trouble, she dies."

"Miserable scum," Clyburn said. "Laying your hands on a nice lady like her."

"Watch the name-callin'," Willard said. "As for her bein'

a lady, I heard tell she and your boss were more than friendly."

"Mr. Shanks aims to marry her."

"Is that so?" Willard laughed. "I wonder if your boss will still want to say 'I do' after he hears that his filly spent all of last night lettin' Fargo, here, lay his hands all over her body."

"What?" Clyburn said.

"As God is my witness," Willard declared.

Clyburn looked at Fargo.

"Hell," Fargo said.

25

"This will end badly," Clyburn said. "You know that, don't you?"

"There was never any other way it could end," Fargo replied.

"I don't know what in hell you two are talkin' about and I don't care," Willard said as he slowly backed out. "Remember. Seven o'clock, or that pretty bitch dies."

Clyburn watched out the door and finally said, "The hayseed is gone." He turned, his hand brushing his holster. "I'd do it now if not for Miss Hatcher."

"You would try," Fargo said.

Clyburn smiled thinly. "I admire a gent with confidence." He turned. "I'm going to get my horse and tie him here so we're ready at seven."

"They said for me to go alone."

"I know the road north. There are heavy woods on both sides. I can shadow you without them seeing."

"It's Marian's life if you're spotted."

"I won't be," Clyburn said, and strode out.

Fargo sighed. He got up, filled his cup with coffee, and placed it on the table. He opened the cupboard, opened all the drawers, searched every nook, and found a hammer behind the stove. Tucking the handle under his belt behind his back, he sat at the table and drank and pondered the state of affairs until hooves clomped and in came Clyburn in his black hat, the conchos on his black gun belt gleaming.

"We have a couple of hours to kill before we have to head out," Clyburn said.

"There's plenty of coffee," Fargo suggested.

Clyburn nodded and stepped to the stove, which put his back to the table.

Slipping the hammer from under his belt, Fargo rose and

cat-crept over and raised the hammer. Some sixth sense caused Clyburn to start to turn and Fargo struck him over the head. The first blow knocked the black hat off and sent Clyburn stumbling into the stove. The second sent him to his knees. Fargo raised the hammer for a third but Clyburn pitched onto his side and didn't move.

"Can't let you put her in more danger than she already is," Fargo said. He cast the hammer to the floor, drained his cup, and departed.

Odds were that Willard and his friends were still in town and wouldn't head for the meeting spot for a while yet. They had plenty of time. If he left now, he could get there ahead of them, and any edge was worth having.

At that time of day the road was heavily traveled. Other riders, wagons, people on foot.

About a mile out to the north, exactly as Willard had said, the woods on the right thinned and there was a half-acre clearing.

Fargo circled around it and concealed the stallion in the trees. Shucking the Henry from the saddle scabbard, he moved to the clearing's edge and flattened in waist-high grass.

Now all he could do was wait.

He set the rifle in front of him, crossed his arms, and rested his chin on his wrist. The heat of the day, the drone of the insects, and his fatigue conspired to make him drowsy. Again and again he dozed off, and would snap his head up and shake it.

The sun slowly described its afternoon sweep of the blue vault of sky.

Fargo had dozed off for the tenth or eleventh time when the clatter of a wagon snapped him back to the here and now.

A buckboard was wheeling into the clearing. Elias was on the seat. Willard rode beside it, a rifle across his saddle. A canvas covered the bed.

Elias turned the wagon so that it faced the road. The bed was now only eight to ten yards from Fargo, and the gate was down. He parted the grass and rose high enough to see two bulges under the canvas. One of the bulges moved and the canvas was pulled aside. Under it were Alonzo and Marian. She was tied and gagged, and Alonzo held a cocked pistol to her head.

Elias wrapped the reins around the brake and said something that Fargo didn't quite catch.

"He'll be here," Willard responded. "He won't let anything happen to her."

"I wish there'd been another way," Elias said. "I don't much cotton to the idea of killin' a woman."

"The bitch slept with him, didn't she?" Alonzo spat. "She has it comin'."

"No one ever has that comin'," Elias said.

"Are you backin' out on us?" Alonzo demanded.

"You know better," Elias said. "He shot Rafer and Milton. He has to answer for them."

Willard said, "Answerin' for is the same as havin' it comin'."

"I suppose," Elias conceded. Taking off his hat, he ran a hand through his shock of hair. "I wish none of this ever happened. I wish we'd let those two bucks be."

"Quit cryin' over spilt milk," Alonzo said. "Anyhow, they were red, and the only good red is one that's dead."

"Amen, brother," Willard said.

"I wish your plan had worked," Elias said to Alonzo, "and Shanks killed him for us."

"You do too damn much wishin'," Alonzo said.

"Amen, again," Willard said.

The sun hung on the western horizon but it would be a while before it set. Out on the road the traffic was lessening. Few people liked to be abroad at night, and folks were either hurrying to town or hurrying away to reach their cabins or camps before dark set in.

"When we're done with him we can get on with lookin' for gold," Elias remarked.

"And when we're done with her," Alonzo said, and jammed his revolver against Marian. She glared and uttered a few words muffled by her gag.

Elias shifted in the seat to look down at them. "You shoot her and that's all you do."

"Don't tell me what to do," Alonzo said.

"I mean it," Elias said. "Killin' her is one thing. I won't abide the other."

"You expect me to let a good-lookin' piece like her go to waste?" Alonzo said, and laughed.

"The other ain't right."

"Listen to you," Alonzo said. "We're about to kill a man and you get on your high horse."

"Molestin' a woman ain't the same," Elias said. "She hasn't done anything to us."

"I tell you what," Alonzo said. "I'll drag her off in the woods so you don't have to hear her squeal."

"No, damn it." Elias turned. "Willard? Why aren't you sidin' with me?"

The big farmer was gazing at Marian and gnawing on his bottom lip. "She sure is an eyeful."

"God, not you, too."

"She's about as pretty a female as I ever saw," Willard declared. "I wouldn't mind a poke before we bury her."

"You think you know someone," Elias said in disgust. "I don't want any part of it, you hear?"

Alonzo snorted. "Fine by us." He reached out and ran his other hand over Marian's hair. "Yes, sir, bitch. You and me are goin' to have a lot of fun before we get around to it."

"How?" Elias asked.

Alonzo snorted again. "How in hell do you think? I'll haul up that dress of hers and haul down my britches and go to it."

"No, I mean how will you kill her?"

"What difference does it make?"

"I don't want her strangled. I don't want her throat slit. Or your blade in her belly. It's not to be slow and painful, you hear me?"

"God Almighty," Alonzo said.

"Willard?" Elias appealed to him. "At least side with me on this. She shouldn't suffer. It should be quick and no pain."

"Quick and no pain," Willard said.

"Weak sisters, the both of you," Alonzo said, and swore.

Fargo had been waiting for Alonzo to take his revolver from Marian's head but the muzzle was still pressed to her temple. He had a clear shot but Alonzo's trigger finger might spasm, sending a slug into Marian's brain.

Willard pulled a pocket watch from his overalls.

"He has half an hour yet."

"Hell," Alonzo said. "I'm sick of waitin' already."

"You picked this clearin'," Elias said. "We could have done it closer to town."

"And have somebody see?" Alonzo scoffed.

They fell quiet.

Fargo chafed at having to wait. Three shots, and it would be over. He raised the Henry to his shoulder and centered the sights behind Alonzo's ear. The moment he could, he would.

Marian tried to move her head but Alonzo cuffed her and snapped, "Be still, whore."

"She's not either," Elias said.

"Will you listen to him?" Alonzo said to Willard. "The way he carries on, you'd think he was smitten."

Willard laughed, and checked his pocket watch. "Ten minutes."

"Damn it," Alonzo said. "It's takin' forever."

Elias bent and picked up a rifle. Sliding to the end of the seat, he slid a leg over.

"Where in hell do you think you're goin'?" Alonzo demanded.

"One of us should be in the trees to cover the other two."

"Stay put," Willard said. "He sees one of us ain't here, he might not come close."

"And we want him close," Alonzo said.

Elias frowned but he set the rifle down and moved back to the middle of the seat. "It wouldn't hurt to take precautions."

"There are more of us and we have her," Alonzo said. "That's enough."

Willard's mount stomped a hoof several times and nickered.

"Hell, even your horse wants it over with," Alonzo said. He meant it as a joke but no one smiled.

"What I don't get," Elias said, "is Fargo blamin' us for his friend. We didn't have nothin' to do with that old man disappearin'."

"A lot of folks have, from what I hear," Willard said.

"My money is on that Shanks feller."

"Bully Bob," Alonzo said, and nodded. "We'll have to watch out for him once we file a claim. He might try to take it from us."

"Let him try," Willard said.

Fargo was ready to try something, himself. He'd noticed a rock. Prying it loose of the soil, he cocked his arm to throw.

26

Fargo knew he was putting Marian Hatcher's life at risk but it was five minutes to seven and when he didn't show up at seven, they would get suspicious. They might take it into their heads to look around, and spot him.

He focused on Willard's horse and threw the rock with all his might at its rump.

The horse did what most any horse would do—it whinnied and bolted toward the road, nearly spilling Willard from the saddle.

"What in the world?" Elias exclaimed.

Alonzo rose partway to see over the side of the buckboard.

Fargo was ready to shoot but Alonzo's revolver didn't leave Marian's head. He hesitated, hoping Alonzo would move.

Up on the buckboard seat, Elias turned and saw him. Their eyes met.

Fargo had to do something and he had to do it *now*—he let out with an Apache war whoop.

Alonzo spun. He started to swing his revolver around, spotted Fargo, and turned to jam it against Marian's head again.

Fargo was quicker. The hammer was already back. All he had to do was stroke the Henry's trigger. At the blast, Alonzo was knocked against the seat. Elias dropped below the seat and frantically tugged at the reins. Fargo tried to aim at him but didn't have a shot. The next moment Elias hollered and the reins lashed, and the team broke into motion.

Out near the road, Willard brought his mount under control and wheeled broadside.

Fargo dropped to his belly a heartbeat before Willard's

rifle thundered and the slug tore through the grass above him. He pushed up, banged a shot at Willard, and went to bang another at Alonzo or Elias.

Alonzo had fallen into the bed and only a knee showed. Elias was whipping the reins, his hat and part of his shoulder showing over the top of the seat.

Fargo didn't have a clear shot at either.

Willard's rifle banged twice and lead peppered the air.

Fargo owed his life to Willard's horse; the animal shied just as Willard fired, and Willard missed. He dropped flat again, expecting Willard to ride down on him. Only Willard had other ideas.

Hammering hooves told Fargo that Willard was galloping after the buckboard.

Swearing, Fargo rose and raced into the forest. He had tied the Ovaro well back and he lost more than a minute in reaching it and swinging astride the saddle. At the clearing he broke into a trot.

Fargo wasn't letting them get away. Not again. Not and have them come after him later. He flew. Confident in the Ovaro, he rounded bend after bend—and they weren't there.

Fargo burned with fury. He'd had them dead to rights. He should have fired sooner. His worry for Marian had cost him.

Yet another bend that Fargo swept around in a flurry of hooves. He was so intent on spotting his quarry off down the road that he almost missed what was nearly under the Ovaro's hooves.

A pair of prospectors burdened with packs must have moved to the side of the road when the buckboard and Willard swept by. Now they were plodding out into the middle again, and into the Ovaro's path. One of them bleated in terror, giving Fargo a split-second warning. He hauled on the reins and missed the first one but the stallion struck the second a glancing blow and sent him stumbling.

"Watch where the hell you're ridin'!" the man he had missed shouted.

Fifty yards brought Fargo to a turn. He spied Willard's horse at the road's edge at the same instant he spied the gleam of sunlight on metal in the trees.

Fearing that the farmer would shoot the Ovaro, Fargo reined to the left. Willard's rifle slammed, and it was a wonder Fargo wasn't hit. He made it into cover and was out of the saddle before the Ovaro came to a stop.

Fargo sought cover behind a small spruce. It occurred to him that Willard was delaying him so Elias and Alonzo could get away. For a bunch of hayseeds, as Robert Shanks called them, they were damned clever.

"You hear me over there, mister?" Willard yelled.

Fargo didn't answer.

"I know you can," Willard said, and by the change in his voice, he was moving.

Refusing to give himself away, Fargo stayed quiet.

"You couldn't let it go, could you? You had to come after us? And all of this over a pair of worthless redskins!"

A shadow darted behind an oak.

"Talk to me, you son of a bitch. Ambushin' us like that."

Fargo centered the Henry to one side of the oak.

"Nothin' to say for yourself, Injun lover? Maybe you're part Injun yourself, as dark as you are."

A lot of people made that mistake. Endless hours in the sun had burned Fargo bronze.

"Say somethin', damn you."

A knob of shadow poked around the oak, and Fargo fired. Crouching lower in case Willard returned fire, he worked the lever to feed a cartridge into the chamber.

"That was damn fine shootin'," the big bigot hollered, sounding amused. "You got splinters in my cheek."

Although he knew he shouldn't, Fargo said, "Stick your head out again and I'll try to do better."

"At last," Willard yelled.

Fargo aimed at the other side of the oak.

"I have a proposition for you," Willard shouted. "Hear me out and we can end this."

It was obvious Willard was stalling, keeping Fargo there so the other two could get away.

"I got lucky at cards last night. I've got forty-three dollars in my poke and it's all yours if you'll give your word that you'll get on your horse and leave and never come back."

Fargo was insulted. "You'll forget about Rafer and Milton?"

"They're gone. What's the use of dwellin' on it?"

"Bring the poke over." Fargo called his bluff.

The silence was itself an answer. Finally Willard thought he was being clever and said, "How about we meet halfway? On the count of three we'll both come out in the open and walk to the middle of the road."

"Go ahead and count," Fargo said.

Willard couldn't keep the delight out of his voice. "One!" he shouted. "Two!" He let half a minute go by. "Three!"

Fargo didn't go into the open.

Willard didn't appear.

"You didn't fall for it," Willard said, and laughed. "What do we do now? Twiddle our thumbs?"

A spike of intuition warned Fargo that something wasn't right. Stalling was one thing. Willard was toying with him. It made him think there was more to it, that Willard had a purpose beyond helping the other two escape. Suddenly uneasy, he glanced over his shoulder.

A figure bounded between trees.

Another was just going to ground.

Fargo flattened and mentally cursed his stupidity. Willard had been stalling, all right, giving the other two time to park the wagon down the road and circle around behind him. He was the dunce of dunces. He kept underestimating them and now they had him hemmed.

"Nothin' more to say?" Willard taunted. "I do. I can't wait to pay you back for my friends. You're a traitor to your own kind, you bastard."

Fargo ignored him for the moment. Elias and Alonzo were the greater threat. Quietly turning, he crawled into a patch of weeds. As motionless as the ground under him, he waited.

"Cat got your tongue?" Willard said. "Let me hear how wonderful redskins are."

Time slowed. Rigid as a board, Fargo heard his own shallow breaths. And something else. The whisper of a stealthy tread. They were close. God-awful close. That they didn't shoot told him they weren't sure where he was.

"I never have understood people like you," Willard blathered on. "Bein' white doesn't mean anything to you, does it? You don't have any pride in your own skin."

Fargo took off his hat and slowly raised his head.

Elias was looking all around, his rifle cocked. Alonzo hadn't shown himself yet.

Fargo sank down. He needed to be patient. He must get them all. If any of them lived, he'd have to go through this all over again. And he would be damned if he'd let that happen.

Furtive movement sparked him into having another look over the weeds.

Elias was farther away.

Alonzo was half-visible behind a tree.

"Where the hell did you get to, mister?" Willard hollered. He sounded closer. "What kind of game are you playin' at?"

Fargo rose onto a knee and brought the Henry's stock to his shoulder. He aimed at Alonzo's chest. One more step, he thought, just one more.

"Look out! There he is!"

It was Willard, at the near edge of the road, bringing his rifle to bear.

Elias spun.

Alonzo ducked behind the oak.

Fargo dropped and rolled.

Willard's rifle cracked, and Elias fired, and bits of green went flying.

Fargo fixed a bead on Willard's mass and stroked the trigger. Willard was jolted but didn't go down and shot back. Fargo jacked the lever, stroked the trigger.

Willard fell onto his backside but he had plenty of life left and banged off two quick shots, the slugs whizzing over Fargo's head.

Fargo ejected, aimed, sent lead at the center of Willard's face.

This time Willard went down like a poled hog and his giant bulk broke into convulsions.

The smack of running boots gave Fargo a heartbeat's inkling that Elias was almost on top of him. Fargo flipped onto his side and fired at the same instant that Elias did. A pain seared Fargo's ribs.

Elias screamed and tottered but gamely pointed his rifle for another try.

Fargo fired, fired again.

Wreathed in gun smoke, Elias melted.

Fargo scrambled to his knees and sought some sign of the last of them.

From behind him came a growl of elation from Alonzo.

"I've got you now, you son of a bitch."

27

Fargo flung himself to the left.

Alonzo was only a few yards away, his rifle trained. He swiveled, the front bead tracking Fargo as Fargo moved, and Fargo did the only thing he could think of—he threw the Henry at Alonzo's head. Alonzo involuntarily ducked, his rifle dipping. Clawing for his Colt, Fargo fanned two shots into Alonzo's chest. Alonzo howled and tried to aim and Fargo shot him in the neck. Alonzo's rifle drooped but Alonzo stayed on his feet, swaying and gurgling blood.

Fargo aimed at Alonzo's right eye and his Colt banged one last time.

Silence fell. His ears ringing, Fargo got up. He had been creased in the side and he was bleeding but he would live. He got his hat, slapped it against his leg, and jammed it on.

His first order of business was to check the bodies. All three were as dead as dead could be. He collected nineteen dollars. "For me to drink to your health," he said to Willard's dulled eyes.

Hastening to the Ovaro, he forked leather and rode down the road to the next bend. Just past it was the buckboard, parked at the side, the canvas stretched over the bed.

Half-afraid of what he'd find, Fargo dismounted and pulled the canvas off.

Marian raised her head and said something through her gag. Tears of happiness trickled down her cheeks.

Fargo tore off the gag.

"Thank God," she said, and pressed her face to his chest and trembled.

Fargo used the Arkansas toothpick to cut the rope around her wrists and ankles. He held her until she was herself again.

"Thank you," she said simply.

"We'll get you to town."

"What about the bodies?"

"They can rot for all I care." Fargo helped her down and over to the Ovaro. He climbed on, offered his arm, and swung her up.

"The buckboard?"

"Someone will come along, wonder what it's doing there, and take it in." Fargo clucked to the stallion.

"You don't seem as happy as I thought you'd be that it's over," Marian said.

"It's not."

"Oh. Shanks." She placed her cheek on his shoulder. "I'm sorry."

"None of it is your doing."

She hugged him and sighed.

Presently Fargo looked over his shoulder to find her asleep. He pressed his left arm to hers so she wouldn't fall off. The miles fell behind them. At length he nudged her and announced, "We're almost there."

Marian blinked and yawned. "Goodness. I didn't mean to pass out on you."

"Did they hurt you any?"

"No. That nasty one, Alonzo, groped me once or twice and whispered things in my ear, but that was all."

The last straight stretch spread before them. So did the long shadows cast by the setting sun.

Ahead, in the middle of the road, sat a man on a bay. He wore a black hat. His gun belt was decorated with silver conchos.

"Hell," Fargo said.

Marian squinted and said, "Who's that? He looks as if he's waiting for someone."

"He's waiting for me."

Her fingers dug into his arm. "Wait. I recognize him now. It's Clyburn. What does he want?"

"I expect he aims to kill me."

"What? Why?"

"Hush now," Fargo said. He shifted the reins to his left hand and placed his right hand on his Colt. When fewer than twenty feet separated the two horses, he came to a stop.

"You got her, I see," Clyburn said. He didn't take his eyes off Fargo.

"What's going on?" Marian asked. "Where's Mr. Shanks? Why are you waiting here?"

Clyburn paid her no mind. To Fargo he said, "My head still hurts."

"You're alive," Fargo said.

"I can't let it pass," Clyburn said rather regretfully. "It's not in me."

"I couldn't either."

Clyburn nodded and climbed down. He stepped clear of the bay and stood with his arms loose at his sides. "Whenever you're ready."

Fargo went to swing down but Marian grabbed him by the arm.

"You're not serious? You're grown men, the both of you."

"Stay out of this, ma'am," Clyburn said.

"I will not," Marian said tartly. "I'm partly the cause, aren't I? You're doing this for Shanks, because he's fond of me."

"That's a part of it," Clyburn said. "Mainly I'm doing it for me."

"But *why*?"

"You wouldn't understand, ma'am."

"Don't treat me as if I'm stupid," Marian said. "Explain it."

Fargo pried her fingers off and climbed down. He arched his back and moved his arms up and down.

"Please don't," Marian said. "Clyburn, I've always thought you were the best of Bob's gun sharks. You're better than this."

"I thank you, ma'am, but we still have it to do."

"You're insane. Both of you. For the last time, this is me pleading."

Clyburn finally looked at her. "Begging your pardon, Miss Hatcher, but you need to shut the hell up now. I used to respect you. Then I heard about you and him." Clyburn nodded at Fargo. "I haven't told Mr. Shanks but I will as soon as I'm done with your lover."

"He's not my—" Marian said, and stopped.

Fargo took a few steps away from the Ovaro.

"I knew it would come to this," Clyburn said.

"Please don't." Marian wouldn't stop.

Fargo shut her out. He concentrated on Clyburn and only on Clyburn. He took in all of the man: his stance, his face, his eyes, and his hands, especially his right hand.

"Whenever you're ready," Clyburn said.

"You're the one who wants this," Fargo replied. "She's right. We don't have to."

Clyburn frowned and glanced at Marian. "Would you do us a favor, Miss Hatcher? On your count of three we'll slap leather."

"How can you even think to ask me? I surely will not be party to a killing."

They were near enough to town that people were staring. A dozen or so had come to the end of the street and were talking in low tones.

"I reckon we'll have to settle this on our own," Clyburn said, and without any forewarning, he swooped his hand to his Colt.

Fargo did the same. Clyburn's Colt boomed first and he felt a slight jar to his left shoulder as if he had been punched. He answered in kind and Clyburn rocked on his boot heels. He fired again and Clyburn staggered and thumbed two shots into the ground. He fired a last time and Clyburn was down.

Fargo looked at his shoulder. His buckskin was torn and his skin was broken but the slug hadn't penetrated. "Twice in one day," he said.

Several of the townsfolk who had been watching ran off.

Marian jumped from the Ovaro. She saw the tear and examined the wound and said in relief, "Thank God. He was supposed to be good."

"He was," Fargo said. "He rushed his first shot." Probably, he reflected, because Clyburn had heard how fast he was reputed to be. He stepped to the body. Clyburn's Colt lay near his outstretched fingers. He scooped it up and wedged it under his belt.

Marian had trailed after him. "What are you doing?"

"Might need an extra soon," Fargo answered. He commenced to reload his.

"This ends it, doesn't it?" Marian said. "Shanks will think twice about causing you more trouble."

"He has plenty of gun hands left."

"He won't come after you," Marian declared. "I'd bet my life savings on it."

"He won't have to," Fargo said. "I'm paying him a visit."

He finished reloading and holstered the Colt and dragged Clyburn to the side of the road. The shots had spooked Clyburn's horse and the bay had gone a dozen yards and was looking back at them. "Take it," he said, pointing.

Marian was mad, her fists clenched. "Excuse me?"

"Take his horse to your place," Fargo directed. "I'm going to the Dunbar." He turned and managed two steps before she was beside him, her fingers wrapped around his wrist.

"You don't have to."

"Yes," Fargo said. "I do."

"Because he was likely to blame for Jim McCullock disappearing? Because of Jareck? Clyburn? What?"

"Let go," Fargo said, and pulled loose. Snagging the reins, he hooked his boot in the stirrup and swung up.

"Please," Marian said.

Fargo leaned on the saddle horn. "You won't have to worry about him anymore. He won't be bothering you."

"It's you I'm worried about." Marian put her hand on his leg. "Don't do it for my sake."

"Not just yours," Fargo said. Bending, he kissed the top of her head.

"Skye, wait!"

Fargo didn't look back.

Word had spread. People stopped and pointed and stared. Those in his way made it a point not to be.

The hitch rail at the hotel was full but no one was out in front. The curtains in most of the rooms were drawn and the few windows where they weren't were empty.

Fargo approached at a walk. He scanned the roofs. He scanned the side streets. As he drew rein there was a suggestion of movement at a curtain on the top floor.

Fargo alighted, loosened the Colt in his holster and the extra Colt under his belt and kept a hand on each. He went up the steps and through the wide doors.

The lobby was empty. Even the desk clerk had made himself scarce.

Fargo wondered how many were waiting for him. Not that it mattered.

Either Robert Shanks would be bucked out in gore, or he would.

28

Two of the gun hands were waiting at the first landing. They didn't try to hide and shoot him from ambush. They stood blocking the stairs, arms at their sides, smirking, confident in their ability and the fact there were two of them.

As soon as Fargo started to climb the taller of the pair said, "That's as far as you come."

"I'm here for Shanks," Fargo said, and continued to climb.

They glanced at one another and the tall one said, "Didn't you hear me? Stop, goddamn it."

"You don't stop," the other one said, "we'll gun you."

Fargo continued to climb, taking his time, poised for the inevitable.

"This is your last warning," the tall one said.

Fargo raised his boot to the next step.

The tall one went for his hardware, and he was fast.

His Remington was half clear when Fargo's Colt crashed.

The other one clawed at his six-shooter but Fargo had the belt gun out and cocked and shot him in the chest. Neither moved after they went down. He stepped over their bodies and started up the next flight.

A figure appeared at the second landing and a six-shooter speared flame and smoke.

Fargo answered in kind, both Colts at once. Impaled, the shooter rose onto his toes, his eyes rolled up in their sockets, and he tumbled.

Fargo stepped out of the way. Cocking both Colts, he climbed. No one shot at him until he was almost to the last floor. The stairwell thundered and holes pockmarked the wall. His own thunder resulted in a limp form collapsing over the rail.

The door to Shanks's suite was shut.

Fargo moved to one side and kicked it. Instantly, three shots resounded and wood slivers sprayed.

In the quiet that followed, a voice asked, "Do you reckon we got him?"

Fargo drew back, slammed his boot against the door next to the latch, and sprang aside as the door flew in.

More shots banged.

"Where is he?"

"I don't see him."

His back to the wall, Fargo groaned.

"I knew it," a man declared, and strode out the door smiling.

Fargo shot him in the face. As the body fell he hurtled through the doorway, shouldering the door aside. He shot at a man by the bar and shot at a man by the window. The man by the bar went down but the man by the window jerked his pistol and fired. Fargo shot him again, and a third dose of lead, and the man clutched at the curtain and brought it down with him.

Gun smoke formed small clouds over the dead. No one else was in the room.

Fargo moved to the bedroom door, once more making it a point not to stand in front of it.

On the other side Robert Shanks called out, "Is he dead, Lucas?"

"No, he's not," Fargo answered.

Shanks swore. "Open that door and I'll blow you to hell. I have a shotgun."

"All the effort you've gone to," Fargo said, "and it comes to this."

"I had this town cowed," Shanks spat. "It was mine, lock, stock, and barrel. Then you came along."

"You shouldn't have killed McCullock."

"How many times do I have to tell you?" Shanks practically screamed. "I didn't touch him."

"I almost believe you."

"I don't give a damn whether you do or you don't."

Turning, Fargo went to a chair in the corner. He tucked the spare Colt under his belt, gripped the chair by its arm, and picked it up.

"What are you up to out there?" Shanks said. "Why is it so quiet?"

Fargo moved to one side of the door. "Here I come," he said, and threw the chair. It hit with a loud splintering of wood and in the bedroom a howitzer went off. The top half of the door exploded, leaving a jagged hole half a yard across.

Fargo could see Shanks breaking the shotgun open to reload. He fired through the hole and Shanks tottered. He fired a second time and the shotgun fell to the floor. He aimed to fire a third time but didn't. Kicking open what was left of the door, he went in.

Shanks was sitting on the floor, his back propped by the bed, gaping in wonder at the scarlet-rimmed holes in his chest. "You son of a bitch," he rasped.

Fargo walked up to him. He cocked the Colt and touched the muzzle to Shanks's brow. "The truth now, and I'll make it quick."

"Go to hell."

"If you'd rather be in pain," Fargo said, and shrugged.

Robert Shanks coughed and a drop of blood trickled from a corner of his mouth. "I told you and told you, you bastard. Rot in hell."

"I'll look you up when I get there," Fargo said, and squeezed the trigger. He sat on the bed and reloaded and stared at the miserable pile that had once been the lord of Tarryall. After a while he holstered his Colt and said, "I'll be damned."

No one tried to stop him from leaving. No heads poked out of other rooms. The desk clerk stayed hid.

Another horse was next to the Ovaro. Fargo sighed and said, "I should have known you wouldn't listen."

"Is he—?" Marian asked.

Fargo nodded. He unwrapped the reins and stepped into the stirrups.

"Then it's over," Marian said. "You can come to my place. I'll take the day off and we'll eat and rest and whatever else you'd like." She grinned suggestively.

"I'd like to," Fargo said. "There's one more thing I have to do."

"What are you talking about? Those men from Kansas are dead. Jareck is dead. Clyburn is dead. Shanks is dead. What else is there?"

"To find out if I'm a fool." Fargo reined next to her, leaned over, and kissed her on the cheek.

"You're coming back, aren't you?"

"You can get on with your life now."

"Oh, Skye," she said.

Fargo put Tarryall behind him at a gallop. It was past midnight when he reached the stretch of Crooked Creek.

Floyd and Lloyd were still up, at their fire drinking coffee, and greeted him with an invite to join them.

"It's good to see you breathing," Floyd said.

"No one has been near your claim," Lloyd said. "We've kept an eye on it like we promised."

Fargo sipped coffee and stared at the mountain across the way. Well up it he saw the same flickering finger of orange he'd noticed on his last visit.

It wouldn't do to go up there in the dark so he slept in the lean-to.

A golden crown adorned the eastern rim of creation when he settled into the saddle and began to climb.

The lingering scent of wood smoke let Fargo know when he was close. Drawing rein, he dismounted and covered the rest of the way on foot.

The camp was on a bench that offered a clear view of Crooked Creek. Fargo could see the lean-to, and Floyd and Lloyd moving about.

He squatted next to the embers and poked about until he uncovered a few red enough to puff into flames. He added kindling and soon had the fire going. Some coffee was left in a pot and he put it on to warm up.

Sitting back, Fargo watched the sun rise. Ordinarily, dawn was his favorite time of the day. But he wasn't in the best of moods and the glow that spread across the Rockies did little to improve it.

When the coffee was hot enough Fargo helped himself to a tin cup left on a rock. He sipped and stared at one of the sleepers for the longest while. Finally he set the cup down. A small stone suited his purpose; he threw it at the sleeper's blanket. The man stirred but didn't wake up. Fargo chose another stone and this time it conked the sleeper on the head.

The man opened his eyes.

"Morning," Fargo said.

"Hell," Jim McCullock said. He pushed his blanket off and sat up and scratched his chin. "I didn't expect this."

"I bet," Fargo said.

Their talk woke the other sleeper, an oldster with a salt-and-pepper beard who rose on an elbow and looked in confusion at Fargo.

"It's all right, Charlie," McCullock said. "He's the friend of mine I told you about."

"Am I?" Fargo said.

"That hurts, pard," McCullock said.

"Does it?" Fargo said.

McCullock got up and came over and hunkered. "You shouldn't ought to be like this."

"What I should do," Fargo said, "is shoot you."

McCullock nodded. "I don't blame you for being a mite upset."

"Just a mite?"

"You have to put yourself in my boots," McCullock said.

"Put me there," Fargo said. "Explain it so I won't feel used."

"Not that," McCullock said. "Never that. You and me go back too far. We're friends, damn it." He paused and gazed down the mountain at the creek. "You know how it was. Shanks wanted my claim. And any claim he set his sights on, he got. I'd about given up hope when you showed up."

"Lucky me," Fargo said.

"No. Lucky me," McCullock said. "You're as tough as they come. Hell, when your dander is up, you're about the meanest son of a bitch alive."

"So you decided to get my dander up."

"I figured that if I was to disappear like all those others, you'd take it personal. I killed a rabbit, smeared its blood on my shirt, cut the shirt with my knife, and left it where I knew you'd find it. Then I snuck up here. I'd already had Charlie bring enough grub to last a month or more."

"Don't forget the will," Fargo said. "That was a good touch."

"I didn't want Shanks jumping my claim once he heard I was dead."

"You set me to kill him or be killed."

Jim McCullock smiled. "It worked, didn't it? He's dead or you wouldn't be here."

Fargo stood. Wheeling on a boot heel, he took a step.

"Wait. Where are you going?"

"We're quits."

"Hold on. I did what I had to. That claim is all I have in this world. You'd have done the same if you were me."

"No," Fargo said. "I wouldn't." He descended into the trees. McCullock hollered his name but he didn't stop. Climbing on the Ovaro, he reined down the mountain. He didn't once look back.

LOOKING FORWARD!
The following is the opening
section of the next novel in the exciting
Trailsman series from Signet:

TRAILSMAN #366
MOUNTAINS OF NO RETURN

*The Mountains of No Return, 1861—where death lurks
around every bend in the trail.*

"We have to be careful how we go about this. It could turn
violent," Lieutenant Charles Rabitoy warned as they drew
rein on a rise overlooking the lights of Hadleyville.

Skye Fargo grunted. He wasn't happy about being there.
He'd signed on to do some scouting for the army, not to
round up deserters.

"Something the matter?" Lieutenant Rabitoy asked.

"Don't mind him," said the third member of their party.
"He hasn't had any whiskey today, and that tends to make
him grumpy."

"Go to hell," Fargo said.

California Jim laughed. Like Fargo, he was dressed in
buckskins. Only where Fargo's were plain and well-worn,
Jim's were covered with red and blue beads and had whangs
a half foot long. Jim's hat wasn't plain like Fargo's, either. It
was broad and high with a curl to the brim. A wide belt

adorned with silver conchos was around his waist, and his holster had silver studs. His bandanna, in contrast to Fargo's plain red one, was bright blue, and it hung halfway to his waist.

"Now, now," Lieutenant Rabitoy said. "I expect you two to get along."

"Jackass," Fargo said.

"What did you just call me?"

California Jim laughed louder. "Pay him no mind, Lieutenant. Skye and me go back a long way. We're the best of pards."

"It doesn't sound like you are to me," Rabitoy said. "And I don't appreciate his slur."

"It's just his style," California Jim said. "Ain't that right, pard?"

"You're a fine one to talk about style," Fargo said. "What was it the newspapers called you that time?" He pretended to be trying to remember, and snapped his fingers. "Now I recollect what it was." He grinned. " 'The prettiest scout on the whole frontier.' "

"Here now," California Jim said. "The scribbler who wrote that was a hack."

"Have you looked in a mirror lately?" Fargo asked.

California Jim made a sound reminiscent of a chicken being strangled. "You can go to hell, too."

"And you two are pards?" Lieutenant Rabitoy said. "Half the time, I get the impression you're ready to shoot each other."

"Shoot Skye?" California Jim said. "Why, I'd rather dig out one of my eyes with my bowie. And the same is true for him."

"Speak for yourself," Fargo said.

Lieutenant Rabitoy shifted in his saddle. "What *are* you so testy about?"

"You," Fargo said.

The young officer sat straighter. "Me? What on earth did I do?"

"You were born," Fargo said.

The pale light of the half-moon revealed Rabitoy's scowl. "I swear. I don't know why the colonel thinks so highly of you. You're impossible to get along with."

"He's not insulting you, Lieutenant," California Jim said. "He's concerned, is all, that you're so—"

"I don't need a translator," Fargo told him, and Jim fell quiet. To Rabitoy, he said, "You're green as grass. You've been at Fort Barker, what, two months?"

"What does that have to do with anything?" Rabitoy said. "I was top in my class at the academy."

"Green as grass," Fargo said again. "Colonel Williams had no business ordering you to bring these men in. You're liable to get yourself killed."

"I'm perfectly competent, I'll have you know," Lieutenant Rabitoy bristled. "Besides, there are only four of them and three of us, and you two are supposed to be cocks of the walk." He said that last part sarcastically.

Fargo sighed. California had been right. He was grumpy, but only because he had a feeling in his gut that things weren't going to go well. The deserters they were after weren't about to go back quietly. Their leader was a man called Mace, who had been in and out of the stockade more times than Fargo had fingers and thumbs. Mace was a bully with an especially mean streak, and he had no respect for authority. "You do know that Luther Mace won't go quietly?"

"He will or else," Lieutenant Rabitoy sniffed. "I'm quite capable of taking care of myself."

"You think you are," Fargo said.

"Enough dallying," Rabitoy said. "Let's get this over with." He gigged his mount.

Fargo followed, and within moments California was beside him.

"You're being kind of hard on the boy, aren't you, pard?"

"Not anywhere near as hard as Luther Mace will be," Fargo predicted.

"That's why the colonel sent us along. To see it doesn't come to that."

"We can only do so much."

"Brighten up, will you?" California said. "Mace and those others have no idea we're after them. We'll get the drop, tie them good and tight, and take them back to the fort, as slick as you please."

"You're not just a little bit worried?"

"Not in the least."

"Liar," Fargo said.

California Jim chuckled.

Fargo didn't find it the least little bit amusing. The men with Mace hadn't enlisted to serve their country. Two had been forced to join the army when they got in trouble with the law. The last was a drunk who wouldn't stop sucking down the bug juice, no matter how many times he was reprimanded.

Fargo looked up. The lights of Hadleyville were less than a quarter of a mile away. He'd been there before. Like many frontier towns, it had more saloons than churches. It also had no law to speak of; the last marshal had been run out on a rail.

"Let me handle this, gentlemen," Lieutenant Rabitoy remarked as they neared the outskirts and slowed. "I'm their superior."

"We have your back," California Jim said.

Fargo would have preferred a bottle. He had only a few days left on his latest scouting stint, and then he'd make up for lost time.

Main Street was a riot of sights and sounds. Every hitch rail was full. Townsmen mingled with off-duty soldiers and cowboys from the nearby ranches.

There was also a handful of Chinese workers from the railroad spur. The Chinese made up a third of the population, but they knew better than to roam at night. The Anti-Chinese League, as they called themselves, had already lynched two workers for no other crime than being Chinese.

"This place sure is lively," Lieutenant Rabitoy said.

"Lively as hell," Fargo drily agreed.

The saloons were doing booming business. Liquor was only part of the attraction. There was gambling, with poker and faro and roulette, and there was the flesh trade, with more soiled doves than in St. Louis.

It was Fargo's kind of town.

"Most of the troopers go to the Bella Donna," California Jim mentioned. "That's where we should stop first."

"Surely Private Mace wouldn't be so obvious," Lieutenant Rabitoy said.

"I doubt he cares much one way or the other," California Jim said. "He's not afraid of being caught."

"That's preposterous. He has to know there are consequences to his rash act."

"Seems to me, youngster," California Jim said, "that you have the habit of assuming other folks think the same as you do."

"Well, don't they?"

"Lordy," California Jim breathed.

"What?"

Probably to be polite, California Jim didn't answer.

Fargo had no such compunction. "The worst mistake you can make is to put your head on someone else's shoulders."

"I'd never be so foolish," Lieutenant Rabitoy declared.

"But you just—" California Jim began, and got no further.

A gunshot crashed and a man in the clothes of a backwoodsman or a farmer backed through the batwings of the nearest whiskey mill. In his right hand was a smoking Smith & Wesson. He kept it trained on the saloon as he sidled to a hitch rail, bellowing, "I'll shoot the first son of a bitch who pokes his head out! Just see if I don't!"

"What's this?" Lieutenant Rabitoy said, drawing rein.

"None of our affair," California Jim told him.

A silhouette appeared in the doorway and the man with the pistol fired. He must have missed because there was no outcry. Spinning, he hurriedly reached for the saddle horn to pull himself up.

The figure came through the batwings, panther-quick, and immediately glided to one side so his back was to the wall. He wore a frock coat and a wide-brimmed black hat and had a Colt in each hand. He fired as the man by the horse spun, fired as the man's legs buckled, fired a final time as the man pitched to his knees and keeled over.

"That will teach you," the shooter said.

Lieutenant Rabitoy reined over. "Hold on there. What's the meaning of this?"

"Who the hell is asking?" the man in the frock coat demanded, coming out into the street. "Oh. A blue belly."

"I'm an officer in the United States Army, I'll have you know," Lieutenant Rabitoy angrily declared. "And I demand an answer."

"Do you, now?"

"Don't trifle with me, sir," Rabitoy warned.

The man in the frock coat still held his Colts, but he didn't point them at Rabitoy. Instead, he said, "In case no one told you, pup, the army doesn't meddle in civilian matters."

"Who are you that you presume to tell me how to conduct my business?"

"Coltraine," the man said. "Jonathan Coltraine."

"Oh, hell," California Jim said.

Lieutenant Rabitoy turned in his saddle. "Do you know this man?"

"I've heard of him," California Jim said. "He makes his living at cards."

"He's a gambler?" the lieutenant said, and shook his head. "His name isn't familiar."

"He was involved in that shooting fracas down to Oro City a while back. He shot three hombres dead and wounded a fourth. Something to do with a woman."

"One of them accused me of sleeping with his wife," Coltraine said.

"Did you?" Lieutenant Rabitoy asked.

"A gentleman never tattles."

Rabitoy colored with resentment. "Your dalliances are irrelevant. It's what you just did before our very eyes that counts. And while you're right in that the army usually doesn't meddle in civilian affairs, you just committed murder on a public street. I'm taking you into custody and turning you over to the federal marshal."

"Like hell you are," Coltraine said. "I'd like to see one of you try."

Fargo had listened to enough. He reined his Ovaro past Rabitoy and said, "How about me?"

No other series packs this much heat!

THE TRAILSMAN

Follow the trail of Penguin's Action Westerns at
penguin.com/actionwesterns